# "YOUR CHOICE OF A LIFE PARTNER IS A MATTER OF SO LITTLE SIGNIFICANCE?"

Clarissa opened her fan and observed her companion more closely.

"Yes. As my offer to you must surely have indicated, I have little wish to make a big project of the undertaking. The only reason I am bothering to learn these social tricks is that I have been told it is the only hope I have of success. If there were an easier way, I would take it."

Clarissa felt her resolve to be civil ebbing away. "As an earl with a secure fortune, I should think you could easily ensnare any impoverished young chit you desired."

Matthew took his eyes from the road to glance at her, his green eyes lit with an emotion she couldn't identify. "So I thought, too, until your impassioned refusal."

"I am rather . . . unlike . . . young women," Clarissa replied ferent aspirations than m

# LORD LANGDON'S TUTOR

## LAURA PAQUET

**ZEBRA BOOKS**
Kensington Publishing Corp.

http://www.zebrabooks.com

*To Paul and to my parents—thanks for believing in me*

ZEBRA BOOKS are published by

Kensington Publishing Corp.
850 Third Avenue
New York, NY 10022

First Printing: October, 2000
10 9 8 7 6 5 4 3 2 1

Printed in the United States of America

# ONE

"You cannot be in earnest," Clarissa cried, shock echoing in every syllable.

"I'm afraid I am," replied her father blandly, extracting a pinch of snuff from a delicately jeweled box. He paused to inhale it, then sneezed, before continuing. "The Earl of Langdon will be arriving in the next few minutes, and you will accept his offer of marriage."

"How am I to accept his offer, when I do not even know the man?" In her agitation, Clarissa jumped to her feet and paced across the faded Aubusson carpet of her father's dim library. There were never enough candles in here, she thought irrelevantly. The room always reminded her of a darkly paneled cave. It was redolent with the mixed and somewhat comforting aromas of pipe tobacco, brandy, and seldom-opened books.

"You must accept it for the simple reason that that is the way marriage is done, as I have explained to you many times." Lewis Denham, Marquess of Wickford, frowned as he regarded his middle daughter. "Do stop wandering about, Clarissa, and listen to reason. I've indulged your romantic notions for four years. At one-and-twenty, don't you think it is time to be realistic?"

"I *am* being realistic," Clarissa said, reseating herself reluctantly in a lumpy chair upholstered in scratchy green brocade. Its loose leg squeaked in protest as she sat down. "I want to marry for love. I do not think it 'realistic' to expect happiness, or even respect, to arise between two people who are forced to live together as the result of a business transaction."

"I think it's very generous of Lord Langdon to make this offer," Clarissa's father replied, ignoring her remarks entirely. "He is one of the richest men in England, and he has a brilliant political career ahead of him in the Lords. He could choose any chit."

"Then why hasn't he? Why should he pick me off the shelf so . . . generously?"

"Because I have gone to the trouble of building up your character and reputation. Langdon and I move in similar circles. He once told me he was in the market for a wife, and that he had no wish to waste his time sipping lemonade and chatting over cakes at Almack's. Since then, I have contrived to mention your name to him at every opportunity. Not that I expected any gratitude from you, which it is evident you do not intend to give me."

"Gratitude!" Clarissa exploded, gripping the wooden arms of her chair. The chair leg gave another indignant squeak. "I am sorry to say it, Father, but why should I feel gratitude when you have done something you knew I would abhor?"

"Because, although you have always been unreasonable, I thought that by now you'd have come to your senses!" Lord Wickford slammed his hand down on the pockmarked surface of his mahogany desk. "Well-bred people have been arranging their marriages for hundreds of years, and England seems to have survived quite well. Why do you find the concept so reprehensible?"

"Why do you find it so attractive?" his daughter fired back. "It certainly did not make your life a joy."

Lewis Denham's face tightened, his pronounced cheekbones becoming even more prominent. "Your mother and I had unusual problems. Just because it was an arranged marriage doesn't mean it was doomed to failure."

"No, it just means that you must force all your children into the same trap to reassure yourself that you and Mama did not suffer in vain." Immediately after the words were out of her mouth, Clarissa realized she had gone too far. She dropped her eyes to her lap and began nervously pleating and re-pleating the sprigged muslin of her skirt, its faded flowers barely visible against their white background.

"That is quite enough, Clarissa," her father said stiffly. "When Langdon arrives, you will see him, and you will accept his suit. I will have no more of this foolishness."

"And if I do not?"

"I will send you to live with your Great-Aunt Agatha."

Appalled, Clarissa stopped twisting her skirt fabric and stared at her parent. "To Yorkshire? To live? With Great-Aunt Agatha? You would throw me out?"

"I am trying to make you see reason. We are not a

rich family. I cannot afford to support you through Season after Season." He rose from his seat and went to stand at the window, where threadbare burgundy curtains stirred slightly in the light spring breeze. His shoulders were slumped, and Clarissa felt a surge of pity for him. It was not his fault, after all, that the family had fallen on hard times. A series of floods and poor harvests had necessitated unavoidable repairs to his estates in Kent. By doing the right thing by his tenants, he had brought the family close to penury.

"If you do not marry, you will be impoverished soon enough after I am gone," he continued. "Alexander will inherit, of course, but I do not think it fair to ask him to maintain a family of his own and his stubborn sister as well." Alexander, Clarissa's younger brother, was currently studying at Oxford.

"You forget, Father, that I have my legacy from Grandmother," Clarissa said, trying desperately to find a way out of this situation. She would come into her small inheritance on her twenty-fifth birthday. Her freedom day.

"That money certainly will not support you for the rest of your life. A few frocks and jewels and it will disappear. Speaking of attire, I suggest you change into one of your more fetching gowns before Langdon arrives."

"I doubt that someone so careless in his choice of wife will give much thought to her appearance." Clarissa's sympathy for her father evaporated under the withering heat of his scorn.

Lewis Denham eyed his daughter steadily across his desk. In the silence that fell between them, Clarissa

could hear the mantel clock ticking ponderously. A
gust of wind blew the scent of new roses into the room.
"Just obey me for once, daughter. I have been patient
long enough."

Clarissa returned his gaze unflinchingly, then rose
from her chair and left the room without a backward
glance.

The Marquess of Wickford leaned back in his
cracked leather armchair and sighed deeply. His willful daughter's attitude did not give him any confidence whatsoever. The next few hours were going to
be devilishly difficult. He'd have to draw on all his
charm to keep Langdon from bolting when that esti-
mable gentleman was confronted by Clarissa in one
of her intractable moods. Probably best to stay just a
minute, then leave them to their own devices, he decided with a gusty sigh. He reached for his snuff box.

A quarter of an hour later, a knock on the door
interrupted Lord Wickford's reflections. Shaftoe, the
butler, entered the library. "A gentleman is here to
see Lady Clarissa. I've put him in the blue salon," he
said in his reedy voice.

"Fine, Shaftoe. Have you informed Lady Clarissa?"

"Yes, my lord. She will be downstairs presently."

In what frame of mind? the marquess asked himself
grimly as he went to meet his colleague and future
son-in-law.


Clarissa walked slowly down the staircase with a
heavy heart. She had gone up to her room to change,
but had been too unnerved to select another gown.

She could not believe that her father had put her in this position. This time, she could see no escape.

Pausing on the landing, she gazed down into the marble foyer and attempted to gather her thoughts. She chastised herself for underestimating her father's determination to marry her off and for overestimating the extent of his patience.

Her dilemma seemed without solution. If she refused Lord Langdon, her father would be furious. She knew he would not hesitate to expel her from the house. And while she had always had contingency plans in that regard, she doubted she could put them into action so soon.

If she accepted Lord Langdon's offer, however, she would spend her life living with a man about whom she knew absolutely nothing, who had chosen her for her background and breeding, not herself. He could be a gambler, a womanizer, or a murderer, for all she knew. Her father, while unlikely to match her consciously to a rake, could quite possibly have been swayed by Lord Langdon's rich estate. Certainly, he hadn't been slow to marry his eldest daughter, Clarissa's sister Emily, to a titled reprobate.

Wearily, Clarissa pushed a stray chestnut-brown ringlet off her forehead. She felt warm, almost feverish, and her stomach was churning. Her misgivings, however, would hold no sway with her father. There was nothing to be done but to concede to his plan. With a resolute sigh, she took hold of the polished oak banister and continued down the stairs, saying a silent prayer that Matthew Carstairs, Earl of Langdon, would not be too appalling.

As she entered the foyer, she noticed the door to the blue salon was open. Moving closer, she saw a tall man with curly dark hair standing before the fireplace, examining the delicate blue Delft tiles that framed the opening. When he did not turn, she realized that her presence was undetected, and took a minute to examine the stranger in more detail.

Even from the back, she could tell that his clothes were of the finest cut. A luxurious brown wool jacket hugged his broad shoulders. Close-fitting fawn pantaloons were tucked into gleaming Hessian boots. Absorbed as he was in his contemplation of the tiles, he stood with the erect carriage of a sportsman. Altogether, a typical man about town.

Her father's voice at her shoulder startled her. "I see you did not bother to change." He scowled at her plain frock. "Well, no matter. Come along." With that, he entered the blue salon. Clarissa followed with the greatest reluctance, scuffing her slipper-clad feet across the room's fitted azure carpet.

Their guest turned and crossed the room as they entered. "Good day, Lord Langdon," said the marquess heartily. "Allow me to present my daughter, Lady Clarissa Denham."

The earl's face lit up with what Clarissa assumed was a well-practiced smile. Her father had mentioned that her suitor was active in the House of Lords. She supposed a ready smile was an asset in political affairs.

"Good morning, Lady Clarissa," he said in a warm, pleasant baritone. "I am Matthew Carstairs."

"Welcome to Denham House," she said automatically, grateful for the years of training that had taught her to be gracious in any situation, no matter how unnerving. And Matthew Carstairs was certainly unnerving.

The curly dark hair she had observed from behind framed a face that reminded her of an Italian sculpture she had once seen at an exhibition. Everything about it seemed to be chiseled from rock: the square chin, the finely modeled cheekbones, even the aquiline nose, which was a shade too sharp to be called handsome. But it was the eyes flashing out from that classical face that made her lose her concentration. A brilliant shade of green, they were large and framed by unnaturally long lashes. At the minute, they were scrutinizing her coolly.

Her father's voice broke into Clarissa's thoughts. "I will leave you two alone to become better acquainted," he said jovially. Without another word, he quit the room. "Not much point in the formality of a chaperon, eh?" Clarissa, despite her best efforts, felt panic rising in her throat. "Please have a seat, Lord Langdon," she said, as she sat down on a dainty but worn Queen Anne chair. He dropped gracefully onto a faded blue damask sofa and continued to eye her.

"Would you care for a cup of tea, my lord?" she said quickly, half rising again to summon the butler. Anyone, even stuffy old Shaftoe, would be welcome as a buffer against this Corinthian with his disarming eyes.

"No, thank you, that won't be necessary. This won't take long, I assure you." He paused, almost imperceptibly. "Will you do me the honor of becoming my wife, Lady Clarissa?"

She stared at him, dumbfounded. The haste of his maneuver left her almost breathless. Was she not to share so much as a cup of tea with him before agreeing to spend the rest of her life as his wife?

He, however, seemed to find nothing unusual in the situation. One leg crossed over the other, one elegantly manicured hand resting on his knee, the gleaming smile still fixed upon his face, he exuded dauntless self-confidence. The implicit arrogance of his offer finally broke through the dreamlike state she had been in since leaving her father's library. She knew with utter certainty that she could not live with herself if she gave this self-important buck yet another reason to walk and talk and act as though the entire world should fall willingly at his gleaming boots. Let her father try to throw her out! If nothing else, she would have the fun of giving this scoundrel his comeuppance.

"I think not, my lord, although I thank you for your kind offer," she replied.

Watching him intently, she thought she saw a brief glimmer of annoyance cross his sculpted features. But just as quickly it was gone, replaced by a look of bland indifference. "Would you mind explaining to me, my lady, the reasons why you are refusing my offer?"

She countered with a question of her own. "Would you mind explaining to me, my lord, the reasons why I should accept it?"

At this remark, there was no mistaking the definite signs of anger on Lord Langdon's countenance. A slow red flush crept up his neck from beneath his snowy white neckcloth and spread across his face.

"In case you are not aware, I control one of the largest estates in all of England," he said in a strained voice. "As the Earl of Langdon, I am able to keep you in the style that that estate allows. But I do not feel the need to embroider my assets at this moment. Your father and I have discussed the advantages of this match at some length."

"You are not marrying my father," Clarissa replied crisply.

"And, it would appear, I am greatly to be envied for not marrying you, either. I have no wish to be saddled with a sharp-tongued wife. Your father assured me that you were a model of womanly virtue."

"And so I am, when I am treated like a woman and not like a horse one wishes to buy at Tattersall's," she cried, goaded to anger for the second time in an hour. A point just behind her temples began to throb painfully, and beads of perspiration broke out on her forehead. "Do you not think it extremely odd to offer for a stranger without even attempting a polite conversation first?"

Matthew Carstairs stared at her. "It was all arranged. There was to be no need for idle courting. I am a busy man, and have no time for such things."

"Well, if you are set on having a wife, you might take half an hour or so out of your crowded itinerary to get to know your next lucky intended before asking for her lifelong commitment." Clarissa rose, shaking like a puppy that has been startled by an unexpected noise. "I am sorry this visit has been a waste of your time, my lord."

Lord Langdon rose, too. "You may be quite sorry.

It's not every day an earl comes calling on a young woman whose family circumstances are, shall we say, not substantial."

The arrogance of it! Clarissa had never been able to understand what drove men to duel and fight, but now she began to comprehend. At the minute, nothing would have pleased her more than to slap Lord Langdon's chiseled face.

"I think I can live with the regret," she said. "Good day, my lord."

"Good day, Lady Clarissa," he said. Silently, he crossed the sky-blue carpet and exited through the open door.

Feeling more ill than ever, Clarissa sat in the cheery blue salon, watching the sunlight flicker on the cream-colored walls, and waited with dread for her father to appear. The excitement of her verbal sparring match with Langdon was gone. Now all that remained was a creeping fear. Would her father send her to Great-Aunt Aggie's this very day?

What a shambles everything was. If only her father had respected her wishes and not interfered. It wasn't as though she had planned to be a burden to him all her life. No matter what he thought, she had no intention of wasting her grandmother's legacy on frills and fripperies.

Having witnessed the debacle of her parents' marriage, she had decided from a very early age to marry for love, or not at all. She did not want her children to live in a stilted atmosphere such as Denham House had had during her own girlhood, where the air had seemed forever rife with unspoken accusations.

Early in life, she had learned to escape her parents' quarrels in the pages of books. She borrowed stacks of romantic novels from Colburn's circulating library, devouring them late at night when she was supposed to be asleep. She adored Maria Edgeworth and cried over the novels of Mrs. Cuthbertson and Mrs. Meeke. Lately, she had become much enamored of the works of Jane Austen and Lord Byron.

Five years ago, she had seen her older sister Emily married off to Simon, Lord Tuncliffe. Emily had always been an obedient child, and she had willingly agreed to the marriage. Her sense of duty extended to writing the family long, chatty letters from the small Tuncliffe estate in Hampshire, talking with forced gaiety about her life with the viscount. But during one of her infrequent visits to Denham House, she had quietly confided to Clarissa that marriage had not been "all that she had anticipated." In fact, it seemed that life with Lord Tuncliffe bore little resemblance to wedded bliss. Tuncliffe, it appeared, had a fondness for gambling and a marked lack of enthusiasm for his own bed.

Emily's misfortune had strengthened Clarissa's resolution to avoid an arranged marriage.

Before making her come-out, Clarissa had pleaded with her father to allow her time to choose her own husband. The marquess, certain that his daughter's unremarkable looks and poor dowry would not have suitors flocking to their drawing room, indulgently gave her permission to enjoy herself fully in the marriage mart. But, he warned her, if it all came to naught he would arrange a match for her, just as he had done for Emily.

Contrary to the marquess' gloomy predictions, Clarissa's bright wit and engaging personality attracted many admirers during her Season. One, the younger son of a respected family, had offered for her three weeks after her presentation at Court. But, while she had enjoyed his company, she knew she would soon tire of his inane chatter. She had gently turned him down.

She proceeded to enjoy herself immensely during the next two Seasons, fending off advances from several gentlemen and turning down another offer from a stuffy baron. None of her suitors had made her heart truly glad.

And now, because of that, her father was going to give her up to the notably meager good graces of her Great-Aunt Aggie.

He was certainly taking his time about it, however.

Cautiously, she went out into the cold marble foyer and tiptoed down an adjoining corridor toward her father's library. The door to that chamber was closed, and she could hear the low murmur of voices within.

Puzzled, she returned to the foyer, just as Shaftoe entered it from the morning room.

"With whom is my father meeting?" she asked the wiry servant abruptly. From his avid expression, she could tell he was burning with curiosity about her own meeting, but she revealed nothing. Ever since childhood, she had delighted in irritating the prissy butler.

"Mr. Farnsworth has come unexpectedly to discuss

some minor matters in Kent needing attention."
Farnsworth was her father's estate manager.

Seeing an opportunity to delay yet another confrontation, Clarissa quickly said to Shaftoe, "Please have the gig brought around. I am going to visit my mother, and will stay with her overnight. And please find Betty and ask her to come to me. I will need her to pack a small valise."

As she climbed the staircase, Clarissa reflected that this ruse would give her some time to think. Her father would never follow her to Grosvenor Square.

# TWO

"You will have to tell him, Clarissa," said Sophia Denham, the marchioness of Wickford, softly. "I know it won't be easy. I wish I could help."

Clarissa smiled before raising a delicate Wedgwood cup to her lips. "Thank you, Mama. But I've made my bed, and now I suppose I must lie in it."

The two women were chatting over cups of chocolate in the marchioness' cozy parlor. With its warm pink silk wall hangings and comfortable sofas upholstered in a matching striped chintz, it was much less formal than the adjoining mahogany-paneled drawing room, and Clarissa much preferred its intimate scale. Here, she and her mother always had their *tête-à-têtes*, exchanging *on-dits*, and laughing merrily over plates of pastries. Today, they were nibbling from a large platter of sugar-dusted biscuits and dense plum cake.

But today, even the lighthearted marchioness had to agree that Clarissa had placed herself in an untenable situation.

"He was just so arrogant, Mama. I wanted to slap his face," Clarissa confided. "If only he hadn't been so precipitate."

"Well, it's done now, my dear." Lady Wickford paused, nibbling nervously on her bottom lip. "If your father insists on sending you away, you know you always have a place to stay under my roof."

"Oh, no, Mama, you know I can't!" Clarissa exclaimed. "It's so very kind of you to offer, but I know you cannot afford to keep me on your allowance. And Father would be livid."

"Frustratingly, you are right," said the marchioness. "Lewis would be furious. I am deep in debt as it is." Clarissa blinked in surprise.

"Maintaining a house, even one as small as this, is not easy," Lady Wickford said by way of explanation. "And then there are Alexander's school fees, which I promised to pay as a condition of our separation. Lewis thought Alexander too slow to benefit to any great extent from higher education. At least in that, he has been proven wrong." Sophia beamed with satisfaction, reflecting on the impressive academic achievements of her son. Then she looked at Clarissa sympathetically. "Would it be so horrible, really, to live with Great-Aunt Agatha?"

Clarissa twisted a corner of her blue challis shawl abstractedly. "It's not that I am ungrateful," she said slowly. "It is very generous of her to offer. But . . . surely you have noticed . . . she can be somewhat . . . difficult?"

"Agatha Denham is a harridan, pure and simple," Lady Wickford said succinctly.

"Mama!" Clarissa cried in mock astonishment.

"Well, it is true, is it not? Do you not remember Lady Billingham's dinner? I thought I would crawl under the table and die when your great-aunt asked, in that particularly grating voice she affects, whether Lady Billingham truly liked having her food cooked to a crisp, or whether she was simply unable to control her kitchen staff." Sophia sighed. "I cannot blame you for not wishing to live with her, as I reflect on the situation. She would have you run off your feet within hours, fetching her combs or her embroidery or a rug for her feet, all the while complaining about her staff, her tenants, and the entire family."

Clarissa smiled. "So you understand my reluctance. You see, I must find a way to survive on my own. I've always had plans in that regard, but I hadn't thought I would need them so soon."

"Plans?" her mother inquired curiously, pouring another cupful of richly fragrant chocolate.

Clarissa took a deep breath. "As you well know, I've always said I would marry for love, or not at all. If I failed to meet the man who could make me love him, I had planned to become a governess or a paid companion."

The marchioness set her cup on the delicate lacquered table with a clatter. "A governess? But surely you don't mean here in London? How could you work as a servant in a home where you may have danced as a debutante or played at cards?"

"No, I would not work in London. As you say, it would be . . . difficult. But do you remember Miss Hilson?"

"Your schoolmistress?"

Clarissa nodded. "In a few months, she is leaving England. She has obtained a position as a governess to the children of Lord Camberton, who has an appointment in the government of Upper Canada."

"Canada!" breathed the marchioness.

Clarissa forced herself to ignore her mother's evident distress and horror. "Miss Hilson wrote me recently that many of the colonial administrators are looking for young women of good breeding to train their children properly. I had decided that, if necessary, I could accompany Miss Hilson. It would break my heart to leave England, but at least I would have a chance to travel."

"And would you enjoy that?" Her mother examined her shrewdly.

"More than I would enjoy spending my life locked to a man I don't love," said Clarissa.

"My dear child, I'm afraid that your father and I have given you a most horrible vision of marriage. All couples who are not madly in love are not as unhappy as we were. Many manage to carve out a tolerable life. I have always regretted that that task was beyond my power."

"Please, Mama, don't blame yourself. If I had been married to Father, I think I would have thrown a vase at him, too."

Lady Wickford looked up from her cup, startled. "How did you know about that?"

"How could I not know? We could hear the crash up in the schoolroom." Clarissa laughed. "Don't look so chagrined, Mama. It all worked out for the best. You have your lovely home here, friends of your own, and four charming children you don't have to discipline who shower you with affection."

"You always have had a knack for seeing the brightest side of things!" Her mother chuckled, then sobered. "Can you see a good side to this dreadful situation with Lord Langdon?"

Clarissa sobered, too. "I wish I could. Maybe things will look better in the morning."

Later that evening, in a bachelor flat in St. James's, two other members of the *ton* discussed Clarissa's abrupt refusal of Lord Langdon's suit.

"I was completely taken aback," said that gentleman, helping himself to Spencer Willoughby's crystal brandy bottle. "Such impudence from the chit. I barely escaped without losing my temper."

"What did you expect?" asked his old friend. "I can't believe you fancy yourself a man of politics. In the Lords, you must need to be somewhat more diplomatic."

"Yes, of course," Matthew Carstairs replied irritably. "But I spent months toadying to her father, talking about my wish to marry, telling him about my estates, my career . . ."

"Am I mistaken, or is it the Marquess of Wickford you wish to marry?" Spencer raised his pale blond eyebrows, and helped himself to another glass of brandy.

"Dammit, Spence, that's almost exactly what she said to me!" Matthew exclaimed with exasperation. "Was that not the course I was supposed to take? Isn't one supposed to get the girl's father's blessing in such affairs?"

Spencer observed his friend's angry countenance, dimly visible in the muted lamplight. "Yes, but it's also rather polite to spend at least a few minutes talking to one's fair intended. It makes the poor woman feel involved in the event, or so I'm told." He tried to keep his face straight, but his eyes danced with mirth.

"But that's the point, Spence. I don't want a woman to feel involved. First of all, I don't have time for courting and wooing and making sheep's eyes at one another at the theater. And secondly, I don't want anyone to feel involved in my marriage. It's strictly a business arrangement."

"Awfully cold of you, my friend."

"It's not cold at all," Matthew retorted fiercely. "Just practical, which is more than I can say for half these moonstruck couples I see in Hyde Park, who probably don't have tuppence or an ounce of good sense between them."

"Well, if it's not the throes of passion that have prompted you to take this sudden plunge into matrimony, what is it? I must admit, I was a bit surprised to hear you'd been out making offers to unknown young damsels."

Matthew sighed heavily, and took a long sip of his brandy. He paused while the rich liquid warmed his throat. "It's not my wish, in particular. It's my uncle's. He is stubbornly determined to see me married before he . . . passes on," he concluded somewhat gruffly.

Spencer, however, was not fooled. "He's worse, then?"

Matthew idly swirled the remaining brandy in his snifter. "Worse some days, better others. The doctors tell me it could be two months, it could be two years. They don't know a thing." He looked up from his glass, sorrow nakedly displayed on his usually impassive face.

Willoughby knew better than to offer sympathy. He chose, instead, to be hearty. "Well, then, you'd better get yourself wed. Try not to be so clumsy with the next chit, though."

"What exactly is it I'm supposed to do with them? I've been so demmed busy in the House these last few years, I've hardly been to a single social event. I've no idea how one is to act at a ball or a musicale. So should I take these young misses for drives in the park? A boat ride on the Thames? I can't exactly bring one for an evening of gaming at White's." He drummed his fingers against the red leather arm of his chair.

"Now don't try to tell me you have no idea how to deal with women. You seemed to have Kitty Pace holding her breath on your every move last year."

"Kitty Pace would hold her breath over any man who gave her as many silly trinkets as I did," Matthew answered sharply. "All it took to keep her happy was anything with diamonds in it and a roll in the sheets as often as possible. Not exactly the approach to use with a young lady of the quality, I assume?"

"You are a man of inestimable intelligence. I perceive that you are naive, but you can be taught." Spencer pursed his lips together and whistled between his teeth. "The question is, by whom?"

"As you seem to have so many answers, what about yourself?"

Spencer laughed heartily. "Much as I would love to

oblige you, Matt, I don't think you'd cut much of a swath squiring me about town on your arm."

Matthew glared at him.

"What you need," Spencer explained, "is someone to practice on. A girl willing to let you try out your courting methods without getting emotionally involved in the proceedings. A tutor, if you will."

"And where am I to find such a chit? Most of them come complete with scheming mamas and a head full of romantic nonsense. When Wickford told me that Lady Clarissa would be willing to marry without any such fuss, it seemed like manna from heaven. I was led to believe we could wrap things up in a businesslike manner. Now I'm incensed with myself for wasting my time on the whole affair."

"Well, why let all that hard work go to waste? It seems to me Clarissa would be the perfect choice. She certainly seems unlikely to fall at your feet in a lovesick swoon."

Matthew stared at Spencer as though Willoughby had just fallen out of a tree. "Are you demented? She's also unlikely to give me any help whatsoever. If I'm not mistaken, only years at one of England's better girls' schools kept her from planting a facer on me today."

Like a barrister presenting his final summation to a jury, Spencer got to his feet and paced across the rich red carpet in front of the fireplace. "She has several excellent reasons to do so. But the primary one, unless I miss my guess, is that she is going to be in very grave trouble with her papa for refusing you. Did you not say he'd almost given up hope of marrying her off, and that the family is in somewhat . . . straitened circumstances?"

"Right on both counts."

"So at this moment, she's probably enduring a dreadful tongue-lashing from her esteemed parent. He'll probably be hounding her day and night to shackle herself to the next human in pantaloons to walk through the door. But if you can convince her father that you're still actively wooing her, it will keep him content for the time being. If nothing else, she'll probably be grateful for that."

Matthew scratched his chin thoughtfully. "You may be right. It certainly couldn't make matters worse. She already hates me."

Spencer thought he detected a hint of regret in that comment, but he merely said, "That seems like a fitting beginning."

# THREE

As quietly as she could, Clarissa opened the front door of Denham House. She hoped that the courage that had helped her turn down Lord Langdon would help her face her father.

Planning to steal quietly across the sunny foyer, Clarissa was a bit disgruntled when Shaftoe appeared.

"Good morning," she greeted the butler briefly.

"Good morning, Lady Clarissa. Have you seen the . . . gift that arrived for you this morning?" His blank face and thin voice told her nothing.

"No, Shaftoe, I've only just arrived. What sort of gift is it?"

Before the servant could reply, Lucinda Denham clattered down the stairs, a flying mass of ribbons, lace and undone hair.

"Rissa, have you seen it? I nearly died when it appeared at the door. It's ever so much fancier than the one Lady Anne Beecher got from that insufferable major last winter. And after you disappeared so suddenly yesterday I was sure that everything was spoiled. I suppose I really don't know much, do I?" Clarissa's sixteen-year-old sister had arrived at the bottom of the stairs, somewhat flushed but exuberant.

If one looked closely one could see the family resemblance between the two youngest Denhams. Where Clarissa was dark, Lucy was fair. Where the former was thoughtful, the latter was impulsive. But they shared the same laughing blue eyes and curious dispositions.

"Well, I suppose you know more than I do, because you know what this mysterious gift is. Where is it?"

"It's in the blue salon. Father said to keep it out of the foyer so it wouldn't cause too much of a commotion with visitors. But he was pleased, I could tell that he was. Come and see!"

Lucy grabbed her sister's hand and tugged her toward the salon. But before they reached the entrance, they heard the door to the library open on its squeaky hinges. Clarissa shot a look of dread at her sister, but Lucy seemed utterly unconcerned.

"Well, well, if it isn't the Incomparable!" Lewis Denham exclaimed with a smile.

"Good morning, Father," Clarissa replied warily.

"A good morning it is, indeed. I must admit I was a bit concerned when you left so precipitately yesterday, but I understand that since I was closeted with Farnsworth, you wanted to tell one of your parents the good news."

"Good news?" Clarissa's mystification and unease grew by the minute. She distrusted her father in these excessively jovial moods. They were always short-lived.

"Don't play the green girl with me, daughter. I know that your interview with Langdon must have gone better than I could have possibly hoped, given your mulish temper. No man sends a gift like that to a woman he's merely marrying for convenience."

"Marrying?" Clarissa repeated weakly.

"Oh, he never got around to asking the question? He will, soon enough. Don't worry, my dear. But wait—you haven't even had time to remove your wrap. Stop pestering her, Lucy, and give her time to freshen up before dragging her around."

"No, it's quite all right, Father. I'm very curious to see my gift." Curious was an understatement. She crossed the foyer and entered the blue salon, trailing a wake of her father, her sister, and even the silent Shaftoe behind her.

Then she gasped.

"Didn't I say it was marvelous?" cried Lucy.

"Marvelous." The events of this unusual morning seemed to leave Clarissa nothing to do but repeat the words of those around her.

On the small writing table next to the fireplace stood an enormous arrangement of rare flowers: orchids, jasmine, orange blossom, and oleander. Their perfume was overwhelming, even in this comfortably proportioned room. Next to the arrangement was a cream-colored envelope. Shakily, Clarissa walked over and picked it up. The seal on the back was that of Matthew Carstairs.

She walked over to the blue damask sofa and dropped onto it with a thump. At least, she thought, the envelope was still sealed. She'd be able to keep his words of derision to herself.

She could scream at him for his impudence. Her father's rage would be even greater—if such a thing were possible—when he realized that his fond hopes of getting an earl for a son-in-law were not only not guaranteed, they were not even within the realm of possibility.

Fuming, she slit the envelope with one well-manicured fingernail and withdrew the contents.

*My dear Lady Clarissa,*

*You may well be perplexed by this rather ostentatious gift, but I hope you enjoy it nonetheless. My friends tell me most young ladies are overjoyed to receive flowers, and I am anxious to curry your regard as I wish to ask a favor of you.*

*I realize that our interview yesterday was needlessly confrontational, and that I must bear at least part of the blame for not couching my offer in romantic terms. As I have long believed that sentiment should play very little part in a marriage arrangement, I have acquired few skills in the intricacies of courting. Lately, however, I have come to realize that I must learn some of the social niceties if I wish to wed. The complication is that I need practice in the skills that other young bucks have polished to a fine sheen. Specifically, I need a young lady who will agree to tutor me without fostering any hopes of her own for a romantic involvement. As you amply demonstrated yesterday that you loathe me, I immediately thought of you as the perfect accomplice.*

*Having seen your father debating in the House on several occasions, I know he is a man who hates to be thwarted, and who can react with some heat if he does not get his way. I suspect that he will be extremely angry*

to learn of the failure of his plan to see us wed, and may
be giving you a dressing-down at this very moment. May
I suggest that you use this bouquet as a means of dissi-
pating his wrath? If you can convince him that I have
not yet offered for you, but mean to continue to press my
suit, it may make your life in his household somewhat
simpler.

After I have learned enough of the proprieties to make
an offer to another young lady, I can simply request an
audience with your father and inform him that "we do
not suit." I believe that is the phrase that romantic-
minded young swains usually use. As we will not have
been formally betrothed, there will be no shame on either
of our parts. And as I will take the responsibility for
ending the arrangement, you will be safe from your father's censure and free to pursue your romantic dreams
elsewhere.

If you agree to honor my request, I would like to begin
this afternoon by taking you for a drive in Hyde Park.
Please reply at your earliest convenience.

Sincerely,
Langdon

Quickly, Clarissa reread the letter to make sure she
had understood this extraordinary proposal correctly.
As her eyes scanned the crisp, creamy sheets, Lucy
burst out impatiently, "For heaven's sake, Rissa, what
does he say?"

Carefully composing her features into a calm mask,
Clarissa raised her face from the letter and took a deep
breath. Her lungs filled with the luxurious scent of

jasmine. "He says he would like to take me for a drive this afternoon," she said simply.

"There you are," crowed her father. "You are to have an earl for a husband and a dollop of romance as well. What more could you desire?"

At the moment, Clarissa reflected, not much more than the reprieve from her father's anger that Lord Langdon's suggestion had given her.

Clarissa had spent the last hour trying on, and then discarding, most of the frocks in her wardrobe, all the while berating herself for her concern over her appearance for a drive with a man she despised and who thought of her as an unusual sort of tutor. Eventually, she had settled on an emerald-green afternoon dress with cap sleeves and a lacy flounce at the hem. The matching parasol, hat, and gloves lay on the table in the foyer. It was a bit too elaborate an ensemble for an afternoon drive, but she had wearied of the effort of making a choice. She knew the outfit suited her and that, she felt, was all that was required for this odd outing.

Now she sat in the blue salon, waiting for Lord Langdon and doggedly trying to focus her attention on a new novel by Maria Edgeworth. But between her unreasonable fears that her costume was unsuitable, and Lucy's innumerable questions concerning her supposed suitor, her concentration had flagged.

"You must know whether he is handsome or not." Lucy had been trying for several minutes to obtain a satisfactory answer to this question.

"Honestly, Lucy, I cannot really say. We did not have very long together." Then, recollecting that she must play the part of the lovestruck girl in order to fool her father, she added, "He does, however, have the most remarkable eyes."

"How are they remarkable?"

"Oh, you'll see when he arrives," her sister replied impatiently. Just then, they heard Shaftoe greeting a visitor at the door. After a moment, he announced Lord Langdon and led him into the salon.

"Good afternoon, Lady Clarissa," the earl murmured, crossing the room to her. After a slight pause, he reached for her hand and raised it briefly to his lips. "What a charming outfit."

Someone had evidently been giving him some lessons already. To her chagrin, Clarissa felt a blush creeping over her cheeks.

"Good afternoon, my lord," she said quickly, and then presented him to Lucinda.

Mrs. Harrison, the rotund housekeeper, bustled through the door almost immediately. "Would you be wanting some tea before your excursion?" Her words were directed at Clarissa, but her curious gaze was focused discreetly on Lord Langdon.

"Yes, thank you, Mrs. Harrison." It would give her a few minutes to study her companion more carefully before finding herself alone with him in his curricle. Today, he was wearing a flawless jacket of blue superfine and beige pantaloons, again with shining Hessian boots. Whatever else one could say about Lord Langdon, Clarissa reflected, one had to admit he had exceptional taste.

Lucy, thankfully, was a fountain of animated conversation, as usual. She questioned Langdon politely
on his estates, his work in the House, his family. "Are
your parents in London for the Season as well?" she
inquired.

"My uncle lives with me. He has not been well
enough to return to the country for some time. My
parents are dead." His voice was curt.

"Oh, I'm sorry to hear that." Lucy's voice trailed
off uncertainly.

"My aunt and uncle took me in when I was a young
boy. My aunt died some years ago." Langdon's voice
was still detached and sharp.

With impeccable timing, Mrs. Harrison arrived with
the tea tray, and the conversation moved to less uncomfortable topics. Soon, the three young people had
finished the array of lemon biscuits and cream pastries
that had accompanied the teapot. "Shall we go out
and enjoy what's left of this fine afternoon?" Langdon
asked Clarissa.

Somewhat cautiously, she agreed.

He seated her in the immaculate white curricle,
loudly gave some instructions to his elderly groom
perched on the back seat, and took up the reins.
Clarissa turned to her companion. "Am I playing my
part correctly?" she asked.

The earl's face was unreadable as they pulled away
from the circular drive in front of Denham House.
The afternoon sun was shining brightly, making Langdon shield his eyes as he eased the curricle into the
passing traffic. "I suppose so. As I said in my letter, I

am unschooled in these matters. I will be depending on your guidance."

She cast an uneasy eye toward the groom behind them. "We should, my lord, perhaps be more discreet when discussing our . . . arrangement."

He glanced away from the road briefly and followed her eye. "Oh, don't be concerned about Phillips. He's as deaf as a post. You have to speak loudly and let him see your lips move. He's oblivious to anything else."

"You certainly chose a practical chaperon for us, my lord," she said with amusement.

"So I thought. Now tell me, exactly, what it is that Phillips will be missing. What does one discuss on one of these aimless drives about the park?"

"Whatever strikes one's fancy, I suppose. The weather, fashion, bits of gossip one has picked up around town."

"Oh my, it sounds enticing."

Clarissa bristled. "I could regale you with my views on the new poetry, or Mary Godwin's theories on the role of women, but I doubt you'd be interested."

His green eyes narrowed. "So you are also well read, in addition to being decorative. Is this the case with all young ladies? Shall I need to make a visit to the circulating library before each assignation to make sure I am up to date on the latest in literature and philosophy?"

The derision in his voice set her already tense nerves on edge. In irritation, Clarissa looked away, staring blankly at a young boy selling flowers on a street corner. "Not necessarily," she replied. "But you may have to polish your manners a bit if you hope to win one of these tender young maids just out of the schoolroom. They are not used to being handled so roughly."

"And you are?"

"I believe a woman should be treated as a whole person, not as a delicate miss to be pampered and coddled. And if being a whole person means being exposed to rudeness and ill-temper, so be it." She turned her eyes back toward her companion.

"More musings from Mrs. Godwin, I assume?" Expertly, he tugged on the reins to guide the horses around a black phaeton that had pulled up in front of a sweet-shop.

"You assume much, sir. It must make you a somewhat annoying negotiator. I find it hard to believe that you are a politician."

He shot a weary glance in her direction. "You are the second person to tell me that in under twenty-four hours." He sighed. "I use the arts of diplomacy and tact when necessary, but I prefer to be open and direct in my personal affairs. Why beat around the bush when it's unnecessary?"

"I must agree with you there, my lord. It is the thing I have found most difficult about my time in society. Twice now, I have been unable to read young gentlemen's intentions correctly, until they have placed me in the embarrassing position of having to turn down their offers."

"So you are on the shelf voluntarily? I rather thought you were too pretty to be left unsought by some young buck."

Clarissa's confusion at his unkind reference to her

single state and his unexpected compliment must have shown on her face, for he continued smoothly, "I fear I must be acting too forward again. Really, if I am going to treat you to flowers and drives and all manner of fripperies, you must start upholding your end of the bargain."

"Very well," Clarissa replied stiffly. "What would you like to know?"

"What other sorts of entertainments should I arrange in the course of a courtship? Drives are all well and good, but occasionally the horses get tired and need a rest."

Clarissa looked off into the distance, idly fingering the ivory handle of her parasol. "Well, an evening at the theater is always amusing."

"Oh my, I was afraid of that. I can't abide the theater."

"Why not, my lord?"

"I see too much poor acting and ill-fitting clothing on the floor of the House to stomach them during my leisure hours," he said with such a sour look that Clarissa laughed out loud.

"What is so amusing?" He looked hurt.

With difficulty, she restrained her mirth. "I am sorry. I have never been to the Lords, but I have seen my father and his friends working themselves up into histrionic rages over some petty issue after a few glasses of port. I'm afraid I understand your point only too well."

"Yes. Well." He seemed supremely discomfited by her amusement. "What else does the Season offer a lovestruck young couple, besides the allure of the stage?"

"There's always Almack's."

"It gets worse and worse! Evenings of insipid conversation, inspections by every ambitious mama from here to Hadrian's Wall, and nothing to fortify the soul but weak lemonade. Please tell me you're enumerating all the most horrifying options first?"

His distress was so real that she bit back another burst of laughter with difficulty. "I hadn't intended to, but that appears to be what I have done. There are other options. What about an excursion to the Tower of London, or an evening at Vauxhall?"

"I suppose those would be interesting," he said with forced enthusiasm. Clarissa appreciated his efforts to be more agreeable, despite the fact that he was obviously a man of little imagination and overly serious disposition.

"If the young lady is interested in antiquities, a visit to the British Museum might be nice. The displays would furnish a ready topic of conversation." Clarissa saw the earl's eyes light up.

"That's the thing!" he exclaimed. "Would such an excursion interest you, Lady Clarissa?"

Pleased to have found an activity they would both enjoy, she said it would, very much.

"Shall we visit it tomorrow afternoon, then? I have not yet had a chance to see the Elgin Marbles."

They agreed on a time, and then lapsed into silence as Lord Langdon guided the curricle into Hyde Park. The carriageways were crowded with barouches, phaetons, cabriolets, and mounted riders, and the scents of warm horseflesh and fresh spring flowers mingled in the air.

"Good Lord, is it always such a crush? The horses can barely stretch their necks." Langdon craned his neck to get a full view of the passing parade.

"It is the most popular time of the afternoon. That's part of the attraction—being able to greet one's friends and catch up on the news of the town." As if to demonstrate, Clarissa waved merrily to a young couple driving towards them in a dangerous-looking high-perch phaeton.

"What a wonderful gown, Clarissa!" cried the tall, blonde woman when the carriages were close enough to permit conversation.

Clarissa introduced the earl to her friends, Lady Anne Beecher and her brother, Lord Harry.

"I am honored to make your acquaintance, my lord," said Anne demurely. Clarissa noted, however, that her friend was taking a painstaking inventory of Lord Langdon's clothes, curricle, and general demeanor. She was certain that she would receive an urgent summons to the Beechers' London residence before the day was out, so that Anne could relieve her obvious curiosity about her friend's companion.

"Do you and your brother drive in the park often?" asked the earl politely.

"Only when Harry can persuade me to avoid the temptations of Oxford Street!"

After exchanging a few more pleasantries, the two couples parted company.

"There, that wasn't so difficult, now was it?" Clarissa asked her escort with a sly smile.

"Idle chatter should not tax any reasonably educated person's intellect," Lord Langdon replied. "Fortunately, your friends appeared to be personable types."

"I'm glad they met with your approval." Clarissa's voice dripped with barely concealed sarcasm. If Matthew noticed it, however, he gave no indication.

The rest of their drive proceeded without any remarkable incident. As he handed her back out of the curricle at Denham House, Matthew briefly raised her hand to his lips as he had done upon their meeting that afternoon. Clarissa felt a frisson of . . . what? She was not certain.

"Just in case anyone is watching from the front window," he explained in a low voice. "It is the required etiquette, is it not?"

"Yes, my lord." Clarissa felt oddly disappointed, then chastised herself silently. Why should she care that this arrogant noble's brief kisses were as much of a sham as his suit? "You are learning quickly."

"For a female, you are proving to be an adequate teacher. It is unfortunate that you did not accept my offer, however. I could have saved you the trouble of schooling me in these useless skills. Until tomorrow." He jumped lightly into the curricle and was gone, leaving Clarissa fuming in the drive.

When she entered the house, she found, not the note from Anne that she had expected, but that redoubtable young lady herself, bursting with anticipation.

"Who was that?" she exclaimed without preamble as Clarissa entered the blue salon, which was still heady with the fragrance of Langdon's overwrought bouquet. "And where did you find him?"

"That," said Clarissa acidly, stripping off her dusty gloves, "was the eminent Matthew Carstairs, Earl of Langdon and king of all he surveys. And to answer your second question, I did not find him at all. My father found him for me."

Anne sobered. "So he has finally followed through on his vow to marry you off?"

Clarissa looked briefly backward into the foyer, then shut the heavy oak door of the salon quietly. "That is what he thinks." Quickly, she described the events of the last two days to her amazed friend.

At the end of the tale, Anne shook her head. "How long do you propose to keep up this charade?"

"As long as it takes to make a suitor out of him. Then he will find himself a willing young miss, and I will be free of him."

"And if he becomes a personable gentleman under your tutelage? Will you consider accepting his offer after all?" Anne's eyes were dancing with laughter.

Clarissa sighed. "No. Two souls meant for each other must know it from the first meeting. Remember when we read Burns? 'But to see her was to love her/Love but her and love forever'? I am sure there was none of that when Lord Langdon laid eyes on me, and I felt nothing of that sort towards him."

"Not even a little? You must admit, he is a pink of the *ton*."

"Perhaps. But an elegant aspect and good connections are not enough for me in a life partner." She stood up and moved restlessly about the room. She picked up a small china figurine from a low table, examined it, replaced it. Then she ran a finger along the bottom of a gilt picture frame, checking for dirt. Of course, there was none.

Anne looked at her friend speculatively. "Don't you think it would be wise to get to know the gentleman a little better before rejecting his suit utterly?"

"My goodness, is my father paying you a fee to badger me?" Clarissa cried with feeling. "No, Anne, I prefer to believe that first impressions are the most telling. If I felt anything for him at all, I would have known yesterday. To me, he is just a way of appeasing my father."

Silently conceding defeat, Anne deftly changed the subject.

# FOUR

As Lord Langdon handed her into his elegant curricle, Clarissa made a vow to be on her best behavior. She did not want this mock courtship to become one long, ceaseless argument.

"My, it's a beautiful day today," she remarked conversationally as he leapt lightly up into the seat beside her. For such a tall man, he was remarkably graceful, she thought. "It seems a bit of a shame to spend the day indoors."

It was indeed a lovely day. The brass fittings of the carriage sparkled in the warm afternoon sun, and a light breeze teased Langdon's dark hair.

"If you would rather, we could go for another drive about the park," he offered reluctantly.

"See, you're learning already!" Clarissa cried. "In your role as suitor, you must try to guess your young lady's wishes and honor them. But in this case, you are mistaken. I'm very curious to see the Elgin Marbles."

"Well then, as your devoted slave, it will be my pleasure to escort you to Bloomsbury," he said. Clarissa did not miss the note of irony in his voice.

Upon reaching Oxford Street, however, they found

themselves trapped in a crush of carriages. As it was such a fine day, half the *ton* was perusing the wares in shop windows. An animated knot of elderly women chatted on the front step of a popular millinery shop. Farther down the block, three impossibly young dandies leaned against the wall of a tobacconist's, avidly surveying the crowd while trying valiantly to give the impression that they didn't care a whit about anything. The atmosphere was rather like that of a country fair.

"What could all these people possibly want to purchase today that they couldn't have purchased yesterday, or the day before that, or the day before that?" Lord Langdon muttered irritably as he gazed at the festively attired crowd. "I've never been able to understand this fascination with parading past the shops every day."

"I must admit, I agree with you."

The earl looked at his companion with unmasked surprise. "I thought that all women were obsessed with shopping. Yesterday, even your friend Lady Anne, who otherwise appeared to be a reasonable creature, seemed barely able to restrain herself from Oxford Street."

"Some women enjoy it, and others do not," Clarissa replied. "Really, Lord Langdon, if you are about to begin a pursuit of young ladies, you must stop thinking of the fair sex as one undifferentiated mass. Otherwise, how will you make a wise choice?" She laughed, and extracted a small lacy fan from her reticule. The breeze had died down in the close confines of Oxford Street, and the day had become rather warm.

"As it doesn't really matter what choice I make, I

suppose I've never taken the time to consider the question." He twitched the reins lightly as he guided his perfectly matched bays across a crowded intersection.

"Your choice of a life partner is a matter of so little significance?" Clarissa opened her fan and observed her companion more closely.

"Yes. As my offer to you must surely have indicated, I have little wish to make a big project of the undertaking. The only reason I am bothering to learn these social tricks is that I have been told it is the only hope I have of success. If there were an easier way, I would take it."

Clarissa felt her resolve to be civil ebbing away. To conceal her ill-temper, she began fanning herself. "As an earl with a secure fortune, I should think you could easily ensnare any impoverished young chit you desired."

Matthew took his eyes from the road to glance at her, his green eyes lit with an emotion she couldn't identify. "So I thought, too, until your impassioned refusal."

"I am rather . . . unlike . . . many other young women," Clarissa replied carefully. "I have different aspirations than most."

"Such as?" His voice evinced little interest, and he turned his gaze back to the road.

"Being treated as a true partner in a marriage, not merely a child-bearing mannequin." She paused. "I take it that the question of children is the reason you have suddenly decided to enter the matrimonial state?"

He was silent for a few moments. Clarissa thought

perhaps he was concentrating on the traffic, but the hesitant way he finally answered her question indicated that he'd given it a great deal of thought.

"If it were up to me, I would have left the question of marriage unresolved for a few more years, at least. I would very much like to build a career in the House of Lords. Lord Liverpool has indicated that I might have potential as a cabinet minister. But such ambitions take time and energy. As I also have the work of overseeing several family estates, I have very little time to spend frolicking in the marriage mart.

"But my uncle has frequently expressed a wish to see me wed in the near future. You see, he is quite ill." He paused, then elaborated briefly. "Consumption."

"I'm sorry." It was inane, but she didn't know what else to say.

"So am I," Lord Langdon said bleakly, returning his full attention to the horses.

Presently, they drew up before the elegant façade of Montagu House, home of the British Museum. As she prepared to descend from the carriage, she felt her white silk glove catch on something sharp.

"Oh heavens," she said, as she realized that the tip of her glove was snagged on a tiny brass nail protruding from the edge of the curricle. "Please forgive me, my lord," she said to Lord Langdon, who was waiting beside the curricle to hand her down. "I'll be but a moment."

Carefully, she removed her glove and detached it from the nail. It did not appear to be damaged, thank goodness. She had but three decent pairs.

The earl let out an almost imperceptible sigh. Not

wishing to make him impatient, she decided to wait to put her glove back on until after he had handed her out of the curricle. Quickly, she extended her bare hand, and felt a small spark of pleasure as his large, warm one closed around it. He guided her smoothly to the ground and released his grip, then looked curiously at her hand.

"What an elegant ring you are wearing," he remarked.

She glanced down at her grandmother's emerald sparkling in the afternoon sun. "Thank you, my lord. It is a family heirloom—the only memento I have of my grandmother, aside from a small legacy she left me. When I was a small child she used to let me play with it, because I was fascinated by the color and the way it caught the light." She paused, remembering. "It is one of my most valued possessions, not so much for its monetary worth as because it reminds me of her. I would never part with it except under the most dire circumstances," she concluded fiercely, as she remembered that she might have to sell the ring to pay for her passage to Canada, if this charade with Lord Langdon failed to forestall her father long enough for her to meet a suitor she could love.

"I hope such circumstances never come to pass," Lord Langdon said with a puzzled look.

Clarissa supposed she had been too forceful in her declamation. She would have to watch herself in the future. With a sigh, she straightened her yellow muslin skirts and mounted the steps leading up to the main entrance of Montagu House.

As they entered the elegant building, Clarissa felt

the familiar excitement and wonder at all the treasures contained in these rooms. She had visited the museum frequently, ever since it had become more widely accessible to the public several years ago. Her first visit had been with her father, who had taken all four siblings there as a special treat. He had been rather pleased at her interest, especially when he contrasted it with the marked boredom the other young Denhams showed.

But, as yet, she had not had time to see the controversial Elgin Marbles. She had followed the debate in the press over the ethics of ripping the pieces from the Parthenon, especially Lord Byron's impassioned rhetoric condemning Lord Elgin's actions. While she agreed with the poet in spirit, Clarissa couldn't help but be glad the treasures were here in London for her to enjoy. It was unlikely she herself would ever travel to Greece.

Thinking of that, she asked Matthew, "Have you ever traveled abroad, my lord?"

"I've been to Ireland, although I suppose that doesn't really count," he said, as they walked slowly through the museum. "I've always been curious to go to the Continent, but with the late war, it hasn't been an option. Have you ever traveled?"

"No. I enjoy learning about faraway places, but I fear I would not be much of a traveler. I get ferociously seasick, even on small boats on the Thames. But I enjoy getting letters from other travelers. My former schoolmistress will soon be working for a British family in the Canadas. She has promised to write me many letters of life in the wilds." She paused. "I have sometimes thought I might go visit her, if circumstances warranted it," she said obliquely.

"Doesn't sound like the sort of place to go as a casual visitor," Lord Langdon remarked.

"No, it doesn't," agreed Clarissa in a strained voice. "Oh look, this must be the room where the Marbles are on display." They had reached an excited crowd gathered before a large doorway. After a lengthy wait, they finally gained admittance to the hall and began slowly walking around the room, admiring the sculptures. They soon found themselves standing before a headless—and unclothed—youth grappling with a centaur.

Clarissa was struck by the utter beauty of the sculpture. Every taut muscle was delineated. The unknown man's legs almost pulsed with athletic strength. And then there was that mysterious knot of flesh just below his torso . . .

Aghast, Clarissa ripped her eyes away from the place she had been staring. To her further horror, she felt a blush creeping up her neck. She had long bemoaned her delicate complexion, which often revealed her thoughts more quickly than words ever could. Even Lord Langdon did not miss her consternation.

"A visit to the British Museum is always . . . educational, wouldn't you say, Lady Clarissa?" To her surprise, she lifted her eyes to see a wide grin on his usually serious face. It changed his aspect utterly. She was so astonished at the transformation that she smiled back at him.

"I believe that a lady should always broaden her mind whenever possible," she replied demurely.

As they both began to laugh, several heads swiveled disapprovingly in their direction. With a supreme effort, they swallowed their mirth and continued their way around the exhibit, studiously avoiding each other's eyes.

"That was quite a display you provoked in there," Clarissa remarked with mock severity as they journeyed back to Denham House. The shopping crowds had thinned, and the late afternoon sunshine had turned the stone facades of Oxford Street golden.

"I provoked it?" Langdon exclaimed, echoing her tone. " 'Twas not I who was looking in unseemly places."

"How could it be unseemly? If the British Museum found the statue fit to display, I cannot believe it to have been in poor taste. Why, there were many other ladies in the room admiring the works."

"And were you admiring what you saw?" A sly smile played about his lips.

"I was merely curious, as any scholar should be."

"Do you truly consider yourself a scholar?" Langdon's voice had lost some of its playfulness.

"Not exactly. How can one be a scholar when one cannot go to university? But I read as much as I can, and I enjoy listening to the conversation in my mother's salon."

"Ah yes. I have heard that your mother is a noted hostess." A faint trace of derision laced its way through Langdon's innocuous words, and Clarissa felt her pleasure in the day draining away.

"Is there something inappropriate in a woman playing hostess to a salon—or reading books, for that matter?" Clarissa stared at her companion's profile, impassive beneath his large beaver hat.

"Not inappropriate. But most women have more important things to do. I suppose your mother, separated from her children, felt the need to fill her days in some way."

"Perhaps Mama would enjoy evenings of intelligent conversation even if she were still living with my father."

"Perhaps," Matthew conceded. "But most women seem content to keep their minds on domestic matters. I have found that when they try to apply themselves to matters of literature, art, and politics, they are inevitably facile." He gave the reins a sharp tug as the curricle approached an intersection. The horses veered smoothly to the right.

"You have a great many opinions on women for someone with a confessed lack of experience with them," Clarissa observed.

"I never said I had a lack of experience with women. Just with young ladies." There was no mistaking the scorn that dripped from the last two words.

"If you are so experienced with so many women, why did you never consider marrying one of *them?*" demanded Clarissa, suspecting that the women of whom he spoke were somewhat less than respectable.

Lord Langdon's answer confirmed her suspicions. "The women I have associated with are vastly amusing creatures with simple tastes, and they have suited my needs admirably," he said stiffly. "And, unlike some females I could mention, they have never felt the need to question me incessantly. As they are . . . somewhat lacking in social graces and gentle birth, however, none of them would make a suitable countess. So unfortunate."

"Ah, so women are bearable as long as they know their place—in your bed, I presume?" Clarissa cried hotly.

"What do you know of such matters?" Lord Langdon shot back with equal heat. "I see that a lack of delicacy is the result of reading too many books. Perhaps that is why most well-bred ladies read them in moderation."

Clarissa bit off a scathing retort as the carriage pulled up before the door of Denham House. For the second time in as many days, she forced herself to alight from the curricle gracefully and politely. Taking a deep breath, she thanked Lord Langdon for the afternoon. "I shall be at your service if you need any further instruction in the art of courting," she said. Unable to resist, she added one last jab. "Judging from your conversation this afternoon, I would say you are still in need of a good deal of practice."

Before Matthew could reply, she spun from the carriage, the heels of her boots grinding in the gravel, and disappeared through Denham House's intricately carved oak door.

As she was taking off her brightly patterned challis shawl and handing it to Shaftoe, the library door creaked. Her father emerged from his lair and came to greet her. "I am glad you have returned, my dear," he said amiably. He was still pleased with her supposed courtship. "I have taken the liberty of inviting young Langdon and his uncle to dinner tomorrow night.

While you were out, I sent a message round to Stonecourt. I can't imagine the old man will come, of course; he goes out so rarely these days. Oh, I also invited Lady Anne and that gangly brother of hers. I thought it might make a pleasant evening for you."

"That will be lovely, Father," Clarissa said listlessly. A whole evening in Lord Langdon's company under the entire household's gaze! How would she manage to hold her tongue?

She must manage somehow, she thought bleakly as she looked at her father's beaming face. The alternatives were much worse.

The following evening, Clarissa sat in her light cambric shift staring drearily into the mirror above her dressing table. She was dreading the dinner to come and was putting off descending to the drawing room until absolutely necessary.

"Have you decided on a frock for this evening, Lady Clarissa?" Betty, her personal maid of many years, broke into Clarissa's gloomy thoughts. "The blue one becomes you so well, and you haven't worn it for ever so long."

Turning from the mirror, Clarissa examined the gowns laid out on the bed for her perusal. Determined not to get into a fuss over her attire as she had the afternoon of her drive with Lord Langdon in Hyde Park, she meekly took her maid's recommendation. "The blue one, then, Betty."

Once she was buttoned into the gown, Clarissa felt measurably more the thing. Betty was right; the cornflower shade made her blue eyes seem especially bright, and the lacy cap sleeves drew attention to her slender arms. The square, low bodice and simple cut marked the gown as being somewhat out of style; her mother had purchased it for her daughter's hopeful come-out some four years ago.

The family fortune, such as it was, did not run to extravagant clothing allowances for every Season, Clarissa reflected as Betty began to dress her hair. But the lack of new gowns didn't bother her unduly. As she had told Langdon, she had no love of shopping, and she preferred owning a few well-made, well-loved gowns to having a closet full of flimsy, faddish dresses. It also pained her to see the way some young women spent money in Town, when it was well known that the tenants on their families' estates could well benefit from the money that just one fine frock would cost.

Clarissa had learned, however, to keep such opinions to herself.

"There, Lady Clarissa, you look just grand," said Betty approvingly as she pulled a few stray ringlets back from her mistress' face. "That young lord will be bowled over when he sees you tonight."

Clarissa looked up at her maid with a guilty start. She had momentarily forgotten her role as the lovestruck chit. Betty was a good girl, but there were no guarantees that a lack of enthusiasm on Clarissa's part wouldn't make its way through the household ranks to her father's ever-vigilant ears. "Oh, I hope he is pleased," she said with a fair approximation of anxiety.

"No doubt of it, milady," Betty replied confidently

as she picked up her combs and pins. "He seems to be a man of taste, for all his stuffy ways. Not that he's too pleased with himself," the maid added hastily. "Being a big nob as he is, I suppose he does have a right to put on airs."

At that moment, Lucy burst noisily into the room.

"Whatever are you doing?" she cried. "They're all down there waiting for you. Lord Harry is boring Lord High and Mighty with stories about fishing, and Father is quizzing Lady Anne about her beaux, and it's all too awful. Please come down!" Lucy sat on the bed with a thump.

That litany of the joys awaiting her did nothing to extinguish Clarissa's dread of the occasion. But it was better to be enjoying one of Cook's fine dinners in a warm, comfortable house than to be working as a companion to a crotchety old lady or as governess to a horde of undisciplined children in some wilderness, she told herself. If she could be pleasant for this one evening, she could extend her period of grace just a bit longer. Perhaps even long enough to meet a gentleman she could love enough to marry.

"You are right, Lucy," she said resolutely, rising from the gilt chair and gathering up her skirts. "Let's go down and join in the festivities."

Everyone had gathered in the drawing room, a large, formal chamber that Clarissa had always disliked. Tall, narrow windows permitted little light to enter, and what few rays did find their way through the heavy gray velvet curtains were instantly absorbed by the walls, which were draped in a depressingly dark shade of burgundy. Long-forgotten ancestors, captured in dull-hued portraits hanging over the fireplace and along the long side wall, seemed to scowl perpetually. The overall effect was not conducive to convivial conversation.

The gathering was as dismal as Lucy had foretold. Anne was still pinioned by her father's barrage of barbed questions.

"I noticed you dancing with the Earl of Danforth at Berringer's rout last Saturday," he was saying as Clarissa and Lucy entered the drawing room. "They say he is a fine horseman."

"I have heard that as well," Anne replied blandly. Then she caught sight of Clarissa, and relief softened her fine features. "Good evening! I had begun to think you had forgotten us all."

Clarissa exchanged brief pleasantries with her old friend and then, remembering her manners and her duty, crossed the room to greet the guest of honor. He was standing with Harry Beecher beneath a portrait of the third marquess, a particularly forbidding-looking individual with huge, bushy black eyebrows. She smiled as she reflected that her ancestor appeared almost formidable enough to cow even the haughty Lord Langdon. Almost.

Matthew's eyes seemed to absorb her from head to toe as she approached. She couldn't be certain, of course, but she thought she detected a gleam of admiration in his glinting green eyes. Despite herself, she felt pleased.

"Good evening, my lord," she said quietly. "I am happy you could be here for our dinner party. And I'm sorry your uncle couldn't join us as well."

A shadow passed across the earl's face. "He sends his regrets. He is most anxious to meet you."

"Is he really?" Clarissa asked with genuine surprise. She could not imagine that Lord Langdon had even told his uncle of her existence.

As if reading her mind, he replied, "I happened to mention yesterday that I had seen the Elgin Marbles. He asked me if I had gone alone, and your name came up in the conversation."

"Oh." She was vaguely disappointed that Matthew hadn't intended to tell his uncle about her.

"One evening we shall have to have you to dine at Stonecourt," he continued. "As Uncle Walter rarely ventures out of the house, it is a rare pleasure for him to meet new people."

Harry had been watching this exchange with interest. "I'm sure he'll be able to make it out of the house to celebrate with you on your wedding day," he put in with his usual awkward eagerness. His comment met with confused silence on the part of the supposedly happy couple.

"Although, of course, you are not yet betrothed. My apologies for being so hasty," Harry amended hastily.

Just then, a brassy bell announced that dinner was ready in the dining room. Matthew and Clarissa exchanged a look of barely disguised gratitude.

Once settled in front of a bowl of steaming turtle soup, Lewis Denham shifted his attention from Anne to Lord Langdon.

"I hear you are going to speak in the Lords tomorrow in favor of relief measures for the poor."

Lord Langdon confirmed that that was so.

"Supporting relief measures does not seem to be the way to gain political favor, my lord," Clarissa put in. "Are not most of the lords opposed to them?"

Her supposed suitor observed her curiously. "Yes, at the minute. The recent marches and protests have made many of them nervous. But several prominent members feel, as I do, that unrest will only continue until true reform is made."

"Ah, so it's a way for you to curry favor and perhaps win yourself a future cabinet post."

Sighing, the earl put his spoon down on his gold-rimmed plate. "It is not as simple as that, Lady Clarissa. The prime minister, for instance, is completely against reform. It was he, remember, who suspended the Habeas Corpus Act and brought in those ridiculous libel laws. These days, one can hardly call Prinny fat without incurring the wrath of the local magistrate."

Lord Harry guffawed loudly.

"But one does not attain high office solely by toadying to the prime minister," the earl continued, tearing apart a fluffy roll and buttering it. "Prime ministers come and go, but the Lords goes on forever. I must be careful not to alienate any potential political allies while advocating reform. It's going to be a very tricky business indeed."

Clarissa noticed that others at the table were observing her with keen interest and, on her father's part, not a little displeasure. Recognizing the signs that she had stepped beyond the pale yet again by venturing into "unladylike" topics, she tried to bring the discussion quickly to a close. "I would be very interested in hearing more about the process at another time, my lord."

"I doubt it, but perhaps we shall explore it further some day when rainy weather keeps us from promenading in the park."

Gritting her teeth at his patronizing manner, Clarissa dipped her spoon into the rich soup and asked Harry about the fishing prospects at his family's country estate this year. Harry's outpouring of information on that topic stifled any need for Clarissa to converse again with Lord Langdon until the pudding arrived.

But as Shaftoe placed glass dishes of fruit on the table, Lord Langdon asked Clarissa, "Have you, by any chance, read the new book by Miss Austen? I have heard it praised prodigiously."

"Yes, I borrowed *Emma* from Colburn's last month, and enjoyed it immensely. The characters, as always, were quite absorbing," she said politely, selecting several plump figs from the dish in front of her. "Yet I believe that *Pride and Prejudice* will always remain my favorite."

"That is the book with the willful heroine, is it not?"

"I wouldn't exactly call Elizabeth willful," Clarissa replied evenly, knowing she was treading onto dangerous ground again. She noted her father staring at her pointedly around an elaborate silver candelabra that stood in the middle of the table, but she paid him no heed. "She had high standards and refused to set them aside, that is all. Did you not think so?"

"I'm afraid I don't read novels. Unlike many people, I really don't have time," the earl said dismissively.

"I suppose buying trinkets for your bits of muslin is a more advantageous use of your precious leisure hours," Clarissa shot back without thinking.

A shocked silence descended upon the table.

Clarissa could hear the wheezy grandfather clock in the hall winding up to strike the hour.

Harry cleared his throat self-consciously.

It was Lord Langdon, astonishingly, who rescued her from her disastrous *faux pas*. "We've had a private joke between us for a few days regarding my somewhat checkered past," he explained smoothly to the amazed dinner party. "Perhaps it is not in the best of taste. It is my fault, really, for starting it."

"Well, well, all in good fun," replied Lewis Denham with a chuckle that indicated he thought the conversational topics of a wealthy earl were above reproach, no matter how declassé they appeared at first. The others around the table visibly relaxed, and the talk moved to less contentious channels.

After dinner, when the ladies had repaired to the blue salon for their customary tea, Anne and Lucy descended on Clarissa like a summer thunderstorm.

"Are you mad?" Anne demanded. "What sort of thing was that—to say? You're going to give the game away for sure!"

"What game?" Lucy asked.

Clarissa gave Anne a warning look, and continued pouring tea. "Why, the game of love, of course," Anne replied simperingly.

"If you ask me, there's no love lost between those two," Lucy said decisively, accepting a slightly chipped cup of tea. "Anyone but our demented father could see that."

Her sister's face fell. "Is it that obvious?"

"Only to those with a minimum of intelligence—or those who aren't blinded by the idea of having an earl as a son-in-law."

Clarissa looked at her younger sister with a mixture of guilt and newfound respect. "I didn't realize you knew."

"I knew as soon as I saw you sitting at your dressing table tonight looking as though you were about to be sent to the guillotine. But what's the confusion? Why not simply tell Father you won't accept the match?"

With some heat, Clarissa told her sister of their father's threat to banish her to Yorkshire and the whims of their great-aunt if she remained unmarried. Lucy was aghast.

"I suppose I'd better hurry up and make up my mind when I have my come-out next year," she said, nervously twisting one of her fair ringlets around her index finger. "Don't worry, Rissa, I can keep a secret when I have to. I won't let Father find out."

Just then, the gentlemen joined them. After a polite interval, Lord Langdon gently but firmly extricated Clarissa from the knot of women and drew her to a quiet corner of the salon.

Out of the corner of her eye, Clarissa could see her father observing them approvingly. His approval would certainly be muted if he could hear their conversation, she reflected.

"Don't let me tell you how to run this charade, but

you certainly seem to have put your foot in it over the pudding," the earl began.

"I wouldn't have been so hasty if you hadn't insisted on provoking me!"

"Provoking you? How?" His brow creased as he evidently reviewed the dinner conversation in his mind.

"By constantly dismissing me and my opinions and my interests as beneath your notice! How do you think it feels to be told in front of an entire table of people that my intelligence is lacking? The gall! You do not know the first thing about me." To her chagrin, Clarissa felt her face flush.

"If I have insulted you, I am sorry." Surprisingly, he did look contrite. "But I did warn you that I was rather ignorant of the ways of young ladies. Most of the—ahem—women of my acquaintance have been rather unschooled. I am not used to thinking of women as my intellectual equals."

Clarissa felt her anger melting away. "But your aunt, certainly, was a woman of good breeding?" she probed gently. "Surely you were able to learn by watching her."

The earl looked away toward the vase on the corner table, which contained the dying remains of the bouquet he'd sent Clarissa, but his eyes did not seem to focus. "My aunt was a wonderful woman but, as my uncle always tells me, she was one of a kind." He paused. "She has been dead now for almost twenty years, and my memories of her are not as clear as they once were."

Clarissa felt as though she had intruded into his private correspondence or his dressing room. To bring his mind back to the present, she belatedly thanked him for rescuing her from her slip of the tongue over dinner.

"It was pure self-interest, in a way," he admitted. "I knew that if your father realized that I was not exactly a besotted young swain, and had no intention of becoming so in the near future, I could lose my teacher. And it would be devilish hard to find another." He grinned, reminding Clarissa of the laughter they had shared at the British Museum.

By the time her father came over to join them, she had firmly put aside her earlier annoyance. She even managed to smile at his unsubtle references to her impending engagement, and noticed that Langdon was equally courteous.

As the evening drew to a close, Clarissa caught Anne's eye as her friend put on her wrap for the journey home. Anne smiled encouragingly. "Good work, my dear," she whispered. "Keep it up."

"I intend to," Clarissa whispered back with a wry smile. "What other choice do I have?"

# FIVE

"I cannot believe you convinced me to come here," Anne remarked as she and Clarissa descended from the creaky Denham carriage. "With your skills of debate and persuasion, perhaps you should be the one on the floor of the House, not Lord Langdon."

"We shall see now, shan't we?" asked Clarissa gaily as the two women approached the entrance to Westminster Palace. In her anticipation, she swung her small reticule back and forth in a most unladylike fashion, and twirled her parasol between her gloved fingers.

Inside the palace, a tall, ramrod-stiff guard raised his sandy eyebrows slightly upon hearing the two young women's request for entrance to the Ladies' Gallery. Most of the women who came to watch debates were of the gray-haired, matronly set. Fortunately, however, he refrained from any disparaging comment, which Anne would have gladly seized as an excuse to retreat.

Seating themselves in the gallery, they gazed down upon a small, august collection of aristocrats milling about in their finery, trading quips and shuffling papers, waiting for the debate to begin. Some had already settled down on the large seats richly upholstered in red velvet and were writing notes on bits of foolscap.

"I still can't make it out, Clarissa," Anne said stubbornly. "Why on earth do you want to spend an afternoon listening to a long, windy speech by a man you despise?"

"I simply wish to see if he is really as sincere as he proclaimed over the dinner table," said Clarissa absently as she scanned the chamber below. "I'm anxious to find some little nugget I can use to deflate his overblown concept of himself when next we meet. Besides, it will make me look even more besotted in the eyes of my father. The longer he believes me infatuated, the longer my life remains peaceful."

Anne glanced at her friend skeptically. They seemed like awfully slim reasons to have gone to all the bother of coming here. Especially on a day when Madame Saulnier was planning to put some lovely new hats in her window display. Anne sighed.

Suddenly, Clarissa's eyes alighted on the reason for their visit, as Lord Langdon entered the chamber, a sheaf of papers in his hand. She noted with reluctant admiration that he was flawlessly attired, as always. His dark blue dress coat hugged his shoulders, and his neckcloth was artfully tied and white as sugar. With a few words to several colleagues, he made his way to a chair and sat down.

"I see the object of your interest has arrived," Anne remarked. "It will be interesting to see such a paragon voicing grave concern for the poor. I must say, he is rather decorative, isn't he?"

Clarissa smiled but did not reply. She kept her gaze fastened on Langdon, her sham beloved. Her curiosity to hear him speak was intense. His condescending comments on Clarissa's shallow interest in politics had had the effect of a challenge on that young woman. She'd show him she was no bufflehead.

As soon as the lords—most of them stout, gray-haired ancients, Clarissa could not help but note—had filed into the chamber, the Lord High Chancellor, Lord Eldon, swept into the room. Even from this distance, he appeared formidable, Clarissa thought. From his bushy eyebrows and wig, to the robe of heavy black silk he wore over his clothes, to the tips of his silver-buckled shoes, he exuded authority. He shouted gruffly for order and sat down heavily on the woolsack, a large pillowlike seat before the throne. After the members had dispensed with a few formalities, Lord Langdon rose and cleared his throat.

Clarissa leaned forward, her hands fidgeting with the fan in her lap.

"My fellow lords," Langdon began, his voice strong and authoritative, giving no sign that he felt his relative youth put him at any disadvantage in this assembly. "I know that most of you are somewhat unsympathetic to the proposition I bring before you today, but please exercise patience and forbearance to listen to my arguments on a subject I believe has truly grave consequences for Britain."

A few of the lords coughed. One wild-haired gentleman sitting toward the back of the chamber settled his head comfortably on an outstretched palm and yawned luxuriously, as if preparing to fall asleep.

"There are many who would say that the poor have no one to blame but themselves for their misery. In some cases, they may be right. There are those unfortunates who drink to excess, who gamble unwisely, who are lazy and shiftless and eager to hoodwink their employers."

"Too true, too true," murmured an angular old woman sitting near Clarissa.

"But the vast majority of England's poor, I hope to convince you today, have been caught in circumstances none of them could have hoped to prevent," Matthew continued. Absently, he pushed a curly brown lock off his forehead, and Clarissa's heart gave a curious little beat she chose to ignore.

"As you know, the long war on the Continent has led to soaring inflation here at home. The high price of bread is a sore point across the country. And, on some estates, lords of the manor have not . . . been able to furnish the necessary upkeep."

Matthew paused. Several of the lords shuffled their papers uncomfortably. Clarissa leaned further forward, fascinated by this subtle display of diplomacy.

"But I am not here today to point fingers. Our duty today, gentlemen, is to improve the lot of England's poorest. Why? Why should we care? Christian charity, of course, demands it. 'Whatsoever you do to the least of these, that you do unto me.' "

Clarissa peered at Matthew, but could detect no irony on his distant face.

"Charity, some say, might best be left to the professionals—the clergymen, that is." Several members chuckled. "But I am here to tell you that there are other reasons to help the most unfortunate of our countrymen. The most important of these is civil peace.

"You cannot have failed to notice the renewed outbreaks of Luddism among the farm laborers. People are afraid for their livelihoods, and rightly so. The Spa Fields riots and the looting that followed them are, I believe, only the beginnings of our problems if we do not act, and act quickly. Unemployed workers are again marching in the streets and agitating in the taverns. If we don't give them some real hope, quickly, I fear they will seek it in the words of Henry Hunt and other orators who will incite them to even greater riots."

Several of the lords, Clarissa noted, nodded in agreement, while others made notes furiously.

Matthew spoke for a few more minutes, then the floor was opened for questions. The first man off the mark was Lord Stowcroft, a red-faced earl whom Clarissa had seen at numerous card parties. She had always vaguely disliked him for his loud voice and rather lewd manners. Various *on-dits* had also given the impression that his estate was one of those falling into disrepair, due in no small part to his love of the gaming table. He would probably be ready to do battle with Matthew after Langdon's comment about landlords who failed in their duties, she reflected.

"My dear boy," Stowcroft began. Clarissa stifled a gasp at this patronizing opening and glanced at Lord Langdon to gauge his reaction. Matthew's face, however, revealed nothing.

"How do you expect to pay for all this munificence?" Stowcroft continued. "The treasury, as you must know, is depleted from the long years of war. Inflation, as you have already mentioned, is rampant. Many of the Lords, as you have already insinuated, have troubles of their own on their estates. Do you suggest we melt down the crown jewels to obtain extra gold sovereigns?" Several of Stowcroft's nearby cronies snickered at this weak quip.

"I am not suggesting that this work will be inexpensive, my lord. I would like to point out, however, that the price of food and clothing for relief measures will be far less than the cost of equipping troops to put down the riots that seem to be breaking out with increasing frequency all across the country. And don't you think, Lord Stowcroft, that it is eminently more just to give the starving workers bread than the tip of a bayonet? I think the erstwhile king of France might even agree with me on that point."

From the murmurs of approval around the chamber, it appeared that many of the members agreed with Langdon as well. And so, although she was loath to admit it, did Clarissa. She was impressed with his speaking ability and more than a little surprised by his evident sincerity.

As the debate continued, Clarissa glanced over at Anne and had to cover her mouth to stifle a laugh. Anne's head had long since fallen against the back of her chair and her mouth was slightly and unbecomingly open. She was fast asleep.

"Wake up, Anne," she whispered, shaking her friend's arm gently. Anne revived with a start and blinked at her friend.

"Shall we depart?" asked Clarissa with a smile. "If we hurry, we might even make it to Madame Saulnier's."

"Was the debate enlightening?" Anne asked, shaking her head as if to clear it while gathering up her belongings.

"Oh, yes," said Clarissa thoughtfully. "Yes, indeed."

As they left the Ladies' Gallery, neither young woman noticed one of the men below look up at them and smile to himself. Normally, Lord Wickford would be displeased to see his daughter here, taking an interest in men's affairs. But as he could only assume this interest was generated by the handsome young Langdon, who was still arguing his cause as they left, Lewis Denham could only rejoice.

"I very much enjoyed your remarks in the House yesterday, my lord," Clarissa remarked.

Matthew looked up at her, startled. "How did you come to be there? The Lords is no place for a lady."

"Why then have the Lords seen fit to maintain a Ladies' Gallery, if we are not welcome?" Clarissa smiled as she helped herself to another piece of shortbread.

Langdon had arrived a few minutes previously, and was taking tea with Clarissa in the blue salon. Shaftoe was playing the unwilling chaperon, as the rest of the household was otherwise occupied. As Clarissa and Matthew chatted, the uncomfortable butler glared out the window at innocent passersby.

"You are not unwelcome, my lady, merely . . ." At

a loss for words, Matthew gave up and popped a jam tart into his mouth.

"My, you seem to have used up all your formidable debating skills yesterday." Clarissa was enjoying herself hugely. Matthew, his mouth full, merely grimaced. "I was particularly impressed with your rejoinder to fusty old Lord Stowcroft. His point had some merit, but your comment put him firmly in his place."

Matthew swallowed. "Stowcroft and his cohorts are going to be a constant obstacle to even the most mild reforms. They have thrown their own fortunes away on gaming and architectural follies, yet they seem very interested in pinching every possible penny for the government. Men who can't keep a watch on their own blunt shouldn't be allowed to make decisions about the country's fortunes." Suddenly he stopped short. "That's not to say that all the lords who are in tight circumstances have been careless with their money. Your father, for instance . . ."

"There's no need to apologize," Clarissa, touched by his awkwardness, cut him off quickly. "Everyone knows it was my grandfather who invested unwisely in some unusual agricultural inventions. And my father had to spend a great deal of money to repair the estates in Kent after that terrible flood. No offense taken, quite honestly."

"Thank you. None was meant," Matthew said uneasily. He picked up his flowered teacup, the dainty china looking utterly incongruous in his large hand. "But as I was saying, Stowcroft and his cronies are going to make my political life quite miserable for the next while. I suspect that some of them have even gone so far as to engage *agents provocateurs*. I cannot prove anything, of course."

"What is an *agent provocateur?*" asked Clarissa, intrigued.

"They are men supposedly engaged by the government to infiltrate protest meetings and urge those gathered toward violence. When the inevitable riot happens, the authorities simply show up, arrest the protesters, and claim that the riot is just one more instance of the unruly poor posing a threat to the country's well-being."

"How shockingly unfair!" cried Clarissa with feeling.

"Yes, it is," said Matthew bitterly. "And why Stowcroft and his ilk cannot understand the wisdom of wisely investing money in relief efforts now instead of recklessly spending on defense later, I cannot imagine. I have been doing some research on reform measures in other countries in order to support my arguments. In Holland, for instance . . ." Suddenly, he stopped, and looked at Clarissa as though he had forgotten she was there. "Please forgive me again. I must be boring you immensely."

Clarissa sighed in frustration. She had been following his train of thought with keen interest. "Not at all, my lord. I find all this political maneuvering highly interesting. Much more so, in fact, than the embroidery and music that are supposed to hold the interest of young women."

"Well, you did warn me you were different. But I must . . . learn more about the ways of more traditional young women," he said vaguely, one eye on Shaftoe's stiff back. "Let us change the topic."

"Very well," said Clarissa resignedly. She had to admit, he was right. Taking a chance that he enjoyed dancing as much as she did, she asked brightly, "Are you going to the Duchess of Landsborough's ball tomorrow evening?"

Matthew took a sip from his teacup and replaced it in his saucer. "I have been invited. I don't often attend such things, but . . . as I am trying to be more sociable these days, I suppose I should go."

"I am going to go myself," she informed him. "The duchess's parties are always delightful."

"Well, I shall see you there, then."

Clarissa glanced nervously at Shaftoe, but he appeared to be paying them no heed whatsoever. Taking a chance, she said quietly to Matthew, "When a gentleman is attending the same function as his chosen lady, it is polite of him to request the evening's first dance before the event, if he has the opportunity."

"Oh, it is? Thank you for the reminder. Will you do me the honor of reserving the first dance for me, Lady Clarissa?"

His offhand manner, indeed his very words, put her in mind of that horrible first meeting here in this room, when he had blithely asked her to marry him. Well, she reflected, at least she now had the upper hand. For a while, at least.

"I would be delighted, my lord," she said, trying to sound enthusiastic. Much to her chagrin, she realized that a small part of her feigned delight was actually quite real. She was more than a little bit curious to find out what it would be like to spin around the floor in Lord Langdon's arms.

Stop that foolishness, she admonished herself. He's an arrogant beast.

"What else should I know about the protocol of a ball?" he asked. "I must admit, I rarely attend these events. When I do, I usually arrive alone, spend most of my time at the card tables, and leave early."

A thought suddenly occurred to Clarissa. "You do know how to dance, do you not, my lord?"

"Oh, yes, Lady Clarissa." She could have sworn his green eyes were twinkling. "I may be antisocial, but I am not entirely unschooled. Just a bit out of practice."

"Well, if you do intend to dance, you must dance with a number of partners. You must not spend your entire time with me."

"You flatter yourself, my dear," he drawled, leaning back against the faded sofa and stretching his long legs before him.

There was that arrogance, back again. Clarissa, painfully aware of Shaftoe's presence, bit back a stinging retort and said merely, "I only meant that young, courting couples sometimes forget the proprieties and spend altogether more time gazing into each other's eyes than is quite proper."

"I shall try to keep that in mind," Matthew said dryly.

Oh, this farce was becoming tiresome, Clarissa thought, as she poured herself another cup of tea and squeezed the juice of a lemon slice into it. How much longer could she keep up this pretense of being a lovestruck chit?

Long enough, hopefully, to find a soul mate of her own, before her father became aware of her deception. Perhaps the gentleman she sought would be waiting on the dance floor at the Duchess of Landsborough's ball.

"May I ask you a favor, Lady Clarissa?" Matthew's rich baritone interrupted her thoughts.

"Of course, my lord."

"That's just what I want to discuss with you. All this 'my lord' business. It just doesn't seem quite right, coming from the daughter of a marquess. Would it be possible for you to simply call me Matthew?" He flashed her one of his rare smiles.

He was the most perplexing man, Clarissa reflected. In one breath, he insinuated that she wasn't worth a second thought, and in the next, he asked her to address him in the most intimate manner. Still, she reflected, it could only help convince her father that they were truly besotted.

"Why yes, I think I could manage that," she said nervously. "Matthew."

My, that did feel strange.

"Spence, I need your help. More specifically, I need your mother's help."

Spencer eyed his friend with unconcealed interest. "I can hardly wait to find out why."

Matthew paced across the bold red carpet before Spencer's fireplace. "Seems I've forgotten one small detail in this courting fiasco. I've told Lady Clarissa that I will dance with her at the Duchess of Landsborough's ball."

"Doesn't sound like you've made a *faux pas* to me," Spencer commented, settling back in his comfortable chair with a contented sigh. He had been sleeping off a very late night at White's when Matthew had rapped sharply on his door. The wings of his chair partially obscured the early afternoon sunlight pouring through the window, making the buzzing in his head a little less intense.

"Spencer, when was the last time you saw me dance?"

"Dance?" Spencer tapped his temple in mock concentration, then winced as his head reverberated. "Can't say as I've ever seen you dance, come to think of it. No, wait. I do believe I saw you take a turn or two around the floor when we were at Oxford. Some rout or other."

"That is probably the last time I have attempted such a thing. I do know the basics, but I need a refresher. And quickly." Matthew drummed his fingers impatiently on the plain wooden mantelpiece. "I seem to remember that your mother is a very good dancer."

"Indeed she is. She never misses a ball of any sort. And I suspect she will be more than pleased to help. Always did have a soft spot for you." Spencer yawned. "You certainly are collecting a rather varied assortment of female tutors-cum-fiancées, Matt. But I must warn you, my mother has no interest in being married to anyone except my father—especially to you."

Despite his obvious anxiety, Matthew gave a bark of laughter. "I've always enjoyed your mother's company. She was wonderfully tolerant of us when we were young bucks just down from Oxford. And I will do almost anything that is required to marry myself off and keep my uncle happy. But become your stepfather I will not."

"Well, since that is settled, onward to my mother's home. Just give me a few minutes first. I desperately need something to slake my thirst."

"Now, Matthew, did you ever learn to waltz?" Lady Riverton, a vivacious matron who looked much younger than her fifty-odd years, stood before him consideringly in her large drawing room. In the last two hours, she had refreshed his memory of the steps of several country dances and the minuet. Despite tripping over the carpet once in his concentration, and mistakenly spinning his hostess when he should have let her return to her place during one of the country dances, he had done tolerably well.

Throughout it all, Spencer had sat on a green velvet sofa, commenting on the proceedings and drinking endless cups of tea.

"I did learn to waltz, years ago, just as it was coming into fashion," Matthew replied tentatively to Lady Riverton's question. "I seem to remember that it is less complicated than some of the other dances we have practiced."

"It is quite simple, in fact, and will make you the toast of the ballroom as well." Lady Riverton pushed a gray curl from her damp forehead. "Spencer, it is lovely that you came to visit—I don't see you nearly often enough, you know—but would you please make yourself useful?"

Spencer straightened his posture with a guilty start. "Of course, dear Mother. Shall I partner our humble student here?"

"Don't be ridiculous," said Lady Riverton, a fond smile for her youngest son tempering her words. "I would just like you to hum a bit of one of the newer waltzes, if you please."

"I'll see what I can do," replied Spencer, launching into a tolerable rendition of a popular Viennese tune. "Will that do?"

"Perfectly, my dear. Thank you." Lady Riverton turned back toward Matthew, who was staring off at a point in the middle distance and feeling most decidedly uncomfortable. "Are you ready to polish your waltzing skills, Matthew?"

"Yes, of course," he said a bit gruffly. "Must say, seems a bit odd to be waltzing with you, though, Lady Riverton. It is rather risqué, is it not?"

Spencer's mother laughed, a marvelous silvery sound that broke the newly arisen tension in the room. "It was so, once upon a time. But it is even permitted at Almack's now, and who are we to disdain what the great patronesses have deemed acceptable? Come here, and I shall show you how to begin."

And so Matthew moved forward to take his friend's mother in his arms, and they began gracefully circling the floor in the drawing room. Idly, he found himself wondering how it would feel to hold Clarissa this way. He suspected it would feel entirely different to dancing with Lady Riverton.

After twenty minutes, Spencer called a halt. "If I hum any more my head shall drop right off my shoulders," he declared. "Looks like you've mastered it anyway, Matt."

"Yes, you are a remarkably adept pupil," Lady Riverton added. "You have what my old dancing instructor used to call natural grace."

"Thank you, Lady Riverton," said Matthew, a faint flush of embarrassment tinting his neck. "And thank you for all your kind help this afternoon."

"Well, anything I can do to launch such a prize as yourself on London's eager young ladies. Now, if I could only convince my young son here to follow your lead."

"Matt has responsibilities, estates, all sorts of things," Spencer broke in quickly, rising from the sofa. "I have no need to rush to the altar yet. Besides, once I'm married and shut away in the country somewhere, you'll never see me." He favored her with his most appealing grin.

"Oh, you will break some young lady's heart some day, I fear," replied his mother tartly. "Maybe you are right. 'Tis best you stay away from the gels until you can behave properly."

"You took the words right out of my mouth, dear Mama."

# SIX

The Duchess of Landsborough was famous, even among the *ton*, for her wildly extravagant soirées. At a masquerade several years ago, Prinny and three of his brothers had all made an appearance, tempted no doubt by the buffet table, which stretched through three rooms and featured no fewer than two hundred dishes.

Clarissa's mother, who was a great friend of the duchess, had told her daughter that their hostess considered tonight's ball "just a small event—nothing unusual, you understand."

It all depended on one's usual style, Clarissa thought as she reached the landing on the first floor of Landsborough House, her father and Anne at her side. The marquess made an immediate dash for the card room. Clarissa and Anne, however, were drawn into the cavernous ballroom like kittens to a bowl of cream.

A bit overawed by the entire scene, Clarissa nervously adjusted the completely decorous neckline of her coral silk dress and gave her elaborately dressed hair a nervous pat. Betty had twined a set of pearls through it tonight, a pretty effect that Clarissa had admired greatly when she first saw it in her dressing room mirror. Now she wondered anxiously if it was still in place. The setting she was about to enter seemed to demand perfection.

Three enormous crystal chandeliers suspended above the room shimmered like evening stars, casting a twinkling light on the hundreds of guests gathered below. The duchess had chosen a Chinese theme for the evening, and silk screens painted with fiery dragons lined one long wall. Black lacquered chairs edged with gold provided seating for those who did not wish to dance. A weighty red-and-gold table held bowls of punch and a variety of pastries. Footmen, splendidly arrayed in red silk outfits closed with black frogs, moved quickly and silently through the chattering throng.

Even Clarissa and Anne, who were well-used to the glittering soirées of the *ton*, paused on the threshold, mouths slightly agape.

"Hasn't anyone ever told you it's impolite to stare?" Lord Langdon's voice beside them made both young women jump. His wide smile took the sting out of his words.

Clarissa noted again how smiling made all the difference to Matthew's features. With his perfectly fitted black evening clothes and artfully tousled dark hair, he was quite an arresting figure. Glancing around the room and spotting a few envious glances, she realized she was not the only woman here to have jumped to that conclusion.

"It's also impolite not to respond to a greeting," the earl prompted gently as he drew them both away from the doorway and into the festive room. "Must I give you some lessons in ballroom behavior?" The grin, if it was possible, widened.

"My, you're certainly in a cheerful mood, for someone who doesn't enjoy social occasions." Clarissa smiled back at him.

"I'm looking forward to an educational evening." When he didn't elaborate, Clarissa realized he was glancing warily at Anne.

"Oh, you needn't be afraid of revealing any secrets to Anne, my lor . . . Matthew. I've told her all about our arrangement."

Matthew's eyebrows rose slightly. But before he could comment, Anne jumped in smoothly.

"She had little hope of keeping it a secret. As soon as I saw her driving in the park with a handsome stranger, I came over to pry the details from her. And I must say, the whole situation has been educational for me as well."

"Oh?" Matthew's brows went up even higher.

"Oh, yes, my lord. I spent a most enlightening afternoon following the debate on poor relief in the House of Lords."

Clarissa laughed. "Your powers of discernment must be even greater than I imagined, Anne, to have gained such enlightenment while fast asleep." The two old friends chuckled.

Before Anne could defend herself with a witty response, a slim blond man, immaculately dressed, came up behind Matthew and clapped him on the shoulder.

"Mustn't keep the newcomers all to yourself, Matt."

He gave both ladies a friendly grin and looked pointedly at the earl.

Langdon gave a exaggerated mock sigh. "Allow me to introduce Lady Clarissa Denham and her friend, Lady Anne Beecher. And this," he informed the two women with a chuckle, "is my old friend, Mr. Spencer Willoughby, who appears as if by magic wherever eligible young women congregate."

"Well, as we are neither, we shall have to take his attentions as a genuine compliment," said Clarissa gaily.

"Neither?" Mr. Willoughby queried.

"There are many young ladies here whose come-out was not as far in the past as was ours," Clarissa informed him. "To many young men's disappointment, Lady Anne's heart belongs to a childhood friend who is temporarily abroad. And I . . ." She stopped, and looked questioningly at Matthew. How exactly should she describe herself?

"There is no need to prevaricate," Matthew said quickly. "We have both found a confidant. Like Lady Anne, Spence knows the whole sordid story."

"I wouldn't exactly call it sordid, Matthew," Clarissa admonished. "Just rather unusual."

"Have it your way," he said indifferently.

"Would you care for a glass of wine, Lady Anne?" Spencer asked.

"Yes, thank you, that would be lovely, Mr. Willoughby."

Spencer directed a speaking look at Matthew. Suddenly, Clarissa had a strong suspicion who had put Matthew up to this whole plan in the first place. If he hadn't been such a pleasant young man, Clarissa would have felt quite justified in being angry at Mr. Willoughby. As it was, she couldn't quite stifle a smile as Spencer cleared his throat and gave his old friend a none-too-subtle nudge with his elbow.

That did it. Matthew started and looked at Clarissa with a slightly shamefaced expression. "May I fetch you a glass of wine as well, Lady Clarissa?"

The urge to smile became even stronger. If the two men didn't leave immediately in search of a footman, Clarissa was certain she would collapse with the giggles. "Yes, thank you, Matthew," she managed to say with only a slight catch in her voice.

With a puzzled look, the earl went off with his friend in search of libations.

When they were safely out of earshot, Anne spoke first.

"They're like one of those traveling marionette shows! You can almost see Mr. Willoughby pulling the strings."

"Well, for my part, it makes me feel a bit better. I'm glad I don't have sole responsibility for making a respectable suitor out of him. It seems his friend has quite adequate training in the social graces. Perhaps between the two of us we can get Matthew up to snuff and married off quite quickly." Clarissa paused. "Do you see any likely prospects?"

"Prospects for what?"

"For Matthew! What we need is a pliant young damsel who will steadfastly refuse to fall in love with him."

"With his looks and position? Not much chance of that. Although he is so dreadfully serious sometimes. That should make the really flighty ones take a second look."

Clarissa was scanning the room covertly. "I think I've found a possibility." She nodded toward a slightly plump young woman sitting on a black lacquered chair. Diamonds sparkled at her pale throat, and emeralds winked from her frizzy red hair, which was already coming loose from its pins. She looked rather uncomfortable in a sumptuous green velvet gown.

"Lady Hester Forrester?" Anne asked. "Well, her family is certainly wealthy enough not to be swayed by Lord Langdon's money. And I have always found her a most agreeable companion, although she is somewhat placid."

"I think a placid young woman would suit Lord Langdon admirably. He seeks only someone to keep his house and bear his children," Clarissa commented as she continued to gaze distractedly about the room, which was already uncomfortably warm. "He has already made it more than plain to me that he does not wish to pursue intellectual conversations with any woman he might marry." Suddenly, her eyes focused on a point across the room. "Of course, he may wish to marry an elegant bride, in which case I may have found the perfect match."

Anne followed her friend's gaze and saw a tall, slim, blue-eyed blonde observing the room coolly from her stance near a set of French doors. Her hair was gathered up from her brow in a stunning topknot, and she wore a luxurious blue silk gown with a daringly low neckline.

"Setting your sights rather high, are you not?

Isabella Larkin is one of the Season's Incomparables, as you well know."

"Well, Lord Langdon is an earl, after all. And from what I've heard, if he is looking at marriage as a business arrangement, he couldn't find a more like-minded partner than Miss Larkin. Mama told me she'd heard Miss Larkin say she'd settle for no one less than an earl, even if he was fifty years old with rotting teeth and gout."

"I'm certain she's been made aware of Lord Langdon's presence already." Anne paused. "But do you think Miss Larkin might be a bit above his touch for his first night out on the marriage mart? Maybe we should break him in gradually."

"The man is not notably lacking in self-confidence," Clarissa remarked dryly.

Just then, Matthew and Spencer returned with four crystal glasses of wine.

"The footmen are being run ragged," Spencer noted. "It took us an inordinate amount of time to find one. Terrible thing, ain't it, to have to work for one's refreshment?" He grinned.

"It saves you gentlemen from the fate of being merely decorative," Clarissa said with a laugh.

"I'd say we have some stiff competition in this assembly, wouldn't you, Matt? The duchess' soirées seem to encourage the ladies to great heights of fashionable elegance. 'I tell you that even Solomon in all his glory was not clothed like one of these.' "

"Well, they certainly 'toil not, neither do they spin'," responded Clarissa thoughtfully.

"Ah, a quick wit and a thorough knowledge of biblical quotations! Rather uncommon among the young damsels of society."

"As I've already explained to Lord Langdon, I'm a bit unusual," Clarissa said with a laugh.

Spencer looked at her shrewdly. "I don't doubt it."

The whining of violin strings alerted the gathering that the music was about to start for a round of country dances.

"I believe that is our cue to take to the floor, if you will do me the honor," said Matthew, extending a hand to Clarissa. She caught a fleeting look pass between Matthew and Spencer, and the latter nodded almost imperceptibly. Once again, she stifled a laugh and struggled not to look at Anne. Thankfully, Spencer spared her the effort by stepping between them to ask Anne to dance.

The four of them moved onto the floor and took their places in a set. Clarissa's cheeks flamed as she noted the curious looks of some of their fellow dancers. Doubtless they were all wondering why the elegant and eminently eligible Earl of Langdon had chosen such a plain-Jane as herself for his first turn on the dance floor in many a month.

Let them wonder, she thought defiantly. He had offered for her, after all. And if they knew what a social disaster that had been, they might not regard him as such a prize specimen.

Heavens, the name marriage mart was so appropriate, she mused. The whole procedure made one feel like nothing so much as a cut of beef offered up for the public's approbation or refusal at a butcher's stall.

As she moved into position, Clarissa caught

Matthew's eye. "Here's to education," she said, as she moved into place opposite him, with Anne beside her and Spencer opposite Anne.

"I wonder if he will be able to dance without Mr. Willoughby guiding his feet," Anne commented *sotto voce* to her friend.

"He assured me he does know how to dance," Clarissa replied, somewhat uncertainly.

The loud opening bars of the music rising from the nearby dais cut off any opportunity for further conversation for the time being.

Clarissa watched apprehensively as the top couple—an older woman and her bored-looking husband—moved through the first figure of the dance. She glanced across the floor at Langdon, but he was staring into the middle distance. Sighing, she made a mental note to remind him to look at her once in awhile. Otherwise, their whirlwind "courtship" would be the object of no little suspicion among the *ton's* gossiping dowagers and their bored daughters.

The top couple held hands briefly, spun through the last steps of the dance, and moved swiftly to the bottom of the set. With a guilty start, she realized it was her turn next. She stepped hesitantly out into the middle of the floor and extended her hand. Lord Langdon came forward and held it in a strong, warm grip.

"Into the fray, my lady," he said with a smile as he swung her around confidently. Her fears melted away as she followed his surefooted lead.

Like matched carriage horses they moved through the intricate steps of the figure. As he drew her near him momentarily, she breathed in the clean, manly scents of soap and starched white linen, along with a musky undertone that made her feel uncomfortably warm. She attributed that warmth, along with her racing heart, to the exertions of the dance.

Soon, he had returned her to her place in the line of women, just as Anne moved into place for her figure with Spencer. Clarissa tried to keep her gaze on the other dancers, but despite her best efforts, her attention moved back to her enigmatic partner. His forehead was beaded with perspiration, but other than that their energetic dance appeared to have affected him little.

"We certainly need not have worried about Lord Langdon's prowess on the dance floor," Anne commented as she returned to her place. "He is certainly holding his own."

"True," Clarissa replied absently, lost in her own musings.

As the music continued, Clarissa found herself swept into the earl's arms several more times. She admitted uneasily to herself that the experience was not altogether unpleasant, although the attention she was garnering from the whispering mamas gathered along the walls of the ballroom did not appeal to her at all. She could see them eyeing her—none too discreetly— behind their fluttering fans, and she reminded herself that she should have expected as much, dancing the first set with the Season's most eligible bachelor.

But despite the gossip, she was having a wonderful time.

As she extended her hand for the final figure, she

gave a tiny sigh of pleasure as she felt Lord Langdon's fingers close around hers once more.

"Are you tired, Lady Clarissa?" he enquired with a kind smile. It was the first time he had spoken to her during the dance.

"A little bit winded, my lord, but nothing to be concerned about," she replied, a little too brightly. Silently, she rebuked herself for enjoying his touch. He was, despite his obvious talents and surface charms, still a self-satisfied Corinthian who was only using her for his own ends. As she was using him for hers, she remembered.

The music soon came to an end, and Matthew escorted her from the dance floor. Clarissa dropped down onto a black lacquered chair. "Would you like a cool drink, Lady Clarissa?" asked Matthew.

Covertly, Clarissa glanced around quickly to see if Spencer had given him any judicious prodding, but Mr. Willoughby and Anne had joined a group in conversation on the other side of the room.

Matthew was definitely learning, and learning quickly. She had to give him that.

"Yes, thank you," she replied.

This time, a silk-clad footman was within easy hailing distance, and they were both soon settled with glasses of refreshing negus.

"What should be my next step, teacher?" asked Matthew. He certainly was in fine fettle tonight. "I suppose I must start trying my wings. If I stay attached to you all evening, people will talk."

"No, of course you must not flutter around me all night," said Clarissa with a slight trace of annoyance.

He needn't have sounded so disgusted by the prospect. "Why not try asking Mrs. Richardson's daughter? All of the Richardson girls are extremely charming. Or perhaps Lady Hester Forrester?" she asked, pointing out the young red-haired woman she had noticed earlier.

Matthew's eyes were scanning the room intently. "There! There is the woman I should like to ask next. Is she one of your acquaintances?"

Clarissa looked in the direction he indicated and was not surprised to find herself gazing at Miss Isabella Larkin.

"No, I'm afraid she moves in somewhat more elevated social circles than I do," she replied, hating the tones of self-deprecation and bitterness in her voice.

Matthew, if he noticed at all, made no remark. "I shall seek an introduction from our hostess, then," he said, and abruptly left her. Watching him stride confidently across the room, she marveled again at his boundless arrogance. Not for a second did he pause to consider that the lovely Incomparable might turn him down. The most frustrating fact of the matter was that he was probably right. Most young women here tonight would consider him a more-than-worthy prize.

Clarissa drank her negus with a somewhat sour feeling. If asked, she could not have explained the reason for her increasingly black mood. Was not her whole purpose in this masquerade to groom Matthew for another marriage proposal? And he was most certainly correct in his assumption that if they spent too much time together, the *ton* would be abuzz. The gossip would not make it any easier on either of them when Matthew finally told her father he had decided not to offer for Clarissa.

That train of thought jolted Clarissa back into a practical frame of mind. If Matthew was going to be as quick about this process as it appeared, she had better start making an effort to get to know some of the unfamiliar eligible young bucks in Town for the Season. She hoped and prayed that a *coup de foudre* would strike her upon gazing on one of them, and soon. Otherwise she would have to start making detailed plans for her escape from her father's determined efforts to marry her off or send her to Yorkshire.

As he had done earlier, Mr. Willoughby seemed to materialize out of nowhere. "I see Matt has begun his search among the gathering's young misses," the blond young man commented as he sat down next to her. He extracted a snowy linen handkerchief from his pocket and mopped his forehead. "Langdon's never been one to waste time. Always seems to have better things on his mind than relaxing and enjoying life."

Clarissa decided she liked Mr. Willoughby a great deal. Perhaps he could be her ticket to freedom? But no, there was no *coup de foudre* here, either. Just a warm feeling of friendship. At least he wasn't as proud as his high-titled friend.

"Aren't you in a similar pickle? I supposed that all young men of a certain age were bound by law to search for a wife." She smiled.

"Just those with a title to perpetuate, which, thanks to

the foresight of my parents in having three healthy sons before me, is not my concern. No, I, unlike Matthew, intend to spend a few more years at least enjoying the variety of delights that London has to offer."

"Are not there delights to be found in marriage as well as in the single state?" she asked slyly.

"Perhaps, but let's just say I prefer to wait for them with breathless anticipation." He grinned, looking incredibly boyish. "Would you care to dance?"

Suddenly feeling that she wanted very much to dance and take her mind off Matthew, Clarissa accepted, handing her empty glass to a passing footman.

As they moved into place for an old-fashioned minuet, however, she found her eyes irresistibly drawn to Matthew and the lovely Isabella. They made a striking couple. Miss Larkin, with her fair hair and peaches-and-cream complexion, was the perfect foil for Matthew's dark looks.

"My, it looks as though Isabella has snagged the prize of the Season already." One of the nearby couples was conducting a conversation in low tones. Clarissa could not see them, but she could hear every murmured word.

"With looks and a dowry like hers, not even the Earl of Langdon is above her touch," answered a male voice. "Wonder what's brought him here? Usually you can't pry him out of White's with a bootjack."

"Perhaps he decided it was time to mix with the common folk for a change," replied the woman with a laugh.

Just then, the music began and Mr. Willoughby led

Clarissa into the opening steps of the delicate minuet. The intricate dance and her partner's lighthearted banter absorbed Clarissa's concentration, until her eyes began to wander back to Matthew and Miss Larkin.

Unsurprisingly, Miss Larkin was a graceful dancer. Her silver-slippered feet seemed barely to touch the ground as Matthew spun her lightly around. She leaned forward and whispered something that made Matthew laugh.

Clarissa, caught up in her observation of the other couple, forgot to watch what she was doing and tripped over the hem of her gown. She pitched forward, and her ankle wrenched awkwardly beneath her.

Stifling a cry of pain and embarrassment, she quickly regained her balance and gazed shamefacedly into Mr. Willoughby's concerned face. She tested her foot and decided that no lasting damage had been done. Physical damage, that is.

"Are you feeling faint? It's deucedly hot in here. Why don't we go out on the terrace and get a bit of fresh air?"

Grateful to him for his tact, Clarissa meekly followed as he led her off the floor and through the wide French doors. Once outside, among several other couples on the terrace, she allowed herself to relax a little. The scent of full-blown roses from the garden below the terrace wafted up to her through the darkness. She breathed in deeply.

"My apologies, Mr. Willoughby," she said. "I was just a bit distracted."

"It does get somewhat disorienting in there, what with all the glitter and everyone spinning about."

Leaving her *faux pas* at that, they moved on to discuss inconsequential topics and several mutual friends. Soon, the music inside subsided and Matthew approached.

"Trying to abduct my fiancée, Spence?" he asked with mock severity.

"The only person who has to believe that is my father, and he's playing cards," said Clarissa somewhat sharply.

"Not anymore he isn't. I suppose he wants to watch his besotted daughter and her ardent swain on the dance floor. If that's the case, I thought it would be prudent to ask you for the next dance."

Again the reluctance. Well, what did she really expect? It wasn't as if it mattered to her.

"Well, since you put it to me in such honeyed tones, how can I resist?" she asked with a slight sarcastic edge.

"I can see I've put a foot wrong again. Obviously I'm not yet past second form in Lady Clarissa's School of Charm."

"My lord, with comments like that, it is unlikely that you will ever graduate."

"If I'm such a sorry case, then I must begin cramming at once. I believe the next dance is about to start."

Rolling her eyes at Spencer, she rose from her bench and took Matthew's arm. Mr. Willoughby, however, did not follow them back into the crowded ballroom. He sat for a few minutes more on a hard stone bench, seemingly thinking deep thoughts.

* * *

On one side of the ballroom, as far as possible from her estranged husband, Lady Wickford watched the colorful assembly from a chair next to the Duchess of Landsborough.

"You've done it again, Julia. The *créme de la créme* has made its way to your doorstep."

"It has, hasn't it?" replied the Duchess of Landsborough complacently. "I believe this is one of my most successful evenings yet. I see even Lewis has made an appearance, and Lord Langdon as well. You don't often see either of them at the tonnish functions, and even more rarely do they favor the ballroom with their presence."

Sophia, who had been apprised of Clarissa's arrangement with Langdon, did not trust herself to speak about the young earl to her friend. She would keep Clarissa's peculiar secret. Not wishing to discuss Lewis Denham either, she merely said, "It must be the spring weather. It brings everyone out-of-doors."

Even the creatures that normally hide under rocks, she added to herself, thinking of her husband. But watching Lord Langdon, she decided that surly metaphor didn't really fit *him* at all. His proposal to Clarissa might have been clumsy and thoughtless, but he certainly seemed to be behaving himself like a gentleman here tonight. He was waltzing with Clarissa, as several younger ladies, including Miss Isabella Larkin, looked on in obvious dismay.

Let them look, thought Sophia proudly. Her daughter was a match for any of those simpering misses. If only her romantic standards didn't get in the way of her good sense sometimes.

With a sigh, Sophia turned her attention back to the Duchess of Landsborough, who had not noticed its absence a whit.

Lewis Denham, on the other side of the ballroom, observed his Clarissa dancing with the earl and permitted himself a brief smile of triumph. He had done well by his daughter, despite her foolish notions. Having assured himself that his plan was succeeding, he returned to the card room. He'd been having devilishly good luck in whist.

# SEVEN

"It's good to see you at the dinner table tonight, Uncle," said Matthew as he took his seat in Stonecourt's ornate dining room. The heavy mahogany table, laid with a fresh white linen cloth, sparkled with freshly polished silver and crystal. In the middle of the table, a bowl of fresh flowers gave off a delicate scent of spring. Such touches were largely lost on Matthew, but his uncle enjoyed dining at a fine table. And since he so rarely dined anywhere but his rooms these days, Matthew had instructed the servants to make the dining room as festive as possible on those days when his uncle's health permitted him to come down for a meal.

"I decided I should make an appearance downstairs once in awhile. Otherwise, people will believe me to be an invalid." Walter Carstairs smiled weakly at his own joke. His nephew, admiring the frail man's brave attitude, smiled along with him but made no comment.

Uncle Walter was dreadfully pale today, Matthew thought. His skin seemed to stretch across his cheekbones as though there wasn't quite enough of it. As they sat down to their soup, a nourishing and fragrant mulligatawny, a wrenching cough frequently convulsed the older man's body. Both uncle and nephew ignored it.

"Did you enjoy yourself at the Landsboroughs' last night?" The older man focused his bright green eyes, so like Matthew's, on his nephew.

Matthew considered briefly. Was "enjoy" the right word? He certainly had not relished the gossiping tongues he had heard whispering behind him wherever he went. His rare appearance seemed to have created a minor social stir—not surprising, in a society where people were forced to stare at the same faces night after night. But still, it had been somewhat annoying. Especially the comments he had overheard while dancing with Clarissa.

"No dowry," one gray-haired dowager had hissed.

"He could have his choice, why would he pick one so long in the tooth?" a young dandy had muttered to a friend.

Really, there were days he wondered why people referred to "polite" society.

His thoughts drifted toward the waltz he had shared with Clarissa. She was a fine dancer, as light and graceful as a bird in his arms. His hand had fit most snugly into the hollow of her trim waist. As he had breathed in the soft, clean scent of her hair, he had wondered idly what it would be like to kiss her.

With a start, he realized his uncle was still waiting for an answer.

"Yes, the ball was mildly agreeable," he conceded.

"And when are you going to invite Lady Clarissa to

dinner? I greatly regretted missing the evening at Denham House."

Matthew was about to evade the issue until he glanced at his uncle's face. The older man was so interested in his nephew's life, and Matthew rarely gave him much insight into it. Suddenly, he felt ashamed.

"Why don't I see whether or not she is free tomorrow night?"

"Yes, that would be fine." Walter Carstairs paused thoughtfully. "How did you meet this young woman, Matthew?"

It was as though Matthew was still back at Eton instead of a grown man with extensive responsibilities. He stifled a chuckle.

"I know her father, Lord Wickford."

"Ah yes. I knew Wickford myself, years ago. Something of a hard man. Dreadful shame about him and his wife."

Matthew made no comment.

"But what about the girl? What is it about her that has captured your interest? You've certainly taken long enough to settle on one."

Matthew sighed. There was no sense trying to delude his uncle, although he knew his relative would be disappointed he wasn't pursuing a love match. "She captured my interest because she is of good family and because her father assured me she would consider marriage a business arrangement."

"A business arrangement?" repeated his uncle, with evident distaste.

"Yes, Uncle Walter," said Matthew wearily. "It is a common practice."

"Perhaps, but you have never been a common sort of person."

Matthew ignored this remark. "Believe me, sir, it is much simpler this way."

"How do you know? Have you tried other types of marriages?" The old man regarded his nephew keenly.

Matthew sighed. "Please, Uncle, I don't wish to discuss it. Aren't you pleased I am actively seeking to wed?"

"I would be more pleased if I thought you were pleased."

"Believe me, this sort of arrangement suits my needs perfectly." Matthew dipped his spoon into the soup.

"Yes, I believe it does." Walter paused again. "But let me give you just one piece of advice, Matthew, and then I'll be silent. You see this bowl of soup here?"

Matthew gave his uncle a puzzled look. "Yes."

"We are eating this very tasty soup for sustenance. Now, one could just sip the broth from the top, and I suppose there would be enough nutrients in it to keep one alive, but barely. The really tasty, nourishing parts of the soup are the meat and vegetables at the bottom of the bowl. You need to eat all of the soup to get the full benefit."

Matthew nodded. He knew there would be some point to this story. His uncle dearly loved using extended metaphors. Matthew had often thought the older man could have been a poet, if he had been so inclined.

"What I'm saying is that marriage is like a bowl of soup," his uncle elaborated.

"Hot, salty, and likely to spill?"

"Don't be witty at my expense," Walter Carstairs admonished with mock severity. "No, marriage is like soup because neither is truly worthwhile unless it is tasted to the depths. You can have just a surface marriage, Matthew. Many people do. But it's much better to share your life with someone heart and soul. Just as I did with my dear Mary." He paused, lost in memories. "Much better," he repeated vaguely.

"Is it much better to spend twenty years pining for someone who can never be returned to you?" Matthew hated himself for the harsh words as soon as they were uttered, but it was too late to take them back.

His uncle, however, merely said, " 'It is better to have loved and lost, than never to have loved at all.' "

"Oh please, Uncle, don't quote that musty old Elizabethan to me. You don't really believe that, do you?"

"I do," Walter said crisply. "You have no capacity for understanding such things, and for that I am sorry. But I would not trade the short time your aunt and I had together for a lifetime with some flighty gel I had married merely for convenience."

Matthew, heartily tired of the conversation, declined to answer. The two men, usually such convivial dinner partners, lapsed into silence as they finished their soup.

\* \* \*

Later that evening, Matthew sat opposite Spencer Willoughby at a somewhat scarred mahogany table in a remote corner of White's, drinking the last drops of a particularly fine claret.

"You did admirably at the Landsborough ball, although I can't believe I had to nudge you to bring the dear girl a drink," Spencer commented. "I happen to know you were trained in the basic arts of courtesy."

"I was distracted."

"By the fair Lady Clarissa?" Spencer's eyes sparkled with merriment.

Matthew gazed gloomily into his glass. "No, of course not. I was on the lookout for menacing mamas, that's all."

"Ah, to have such problems. As the fourth son of a mere baron, I am rarely troubled by such attentions." Spencer glanced around the small, crowded room. It was hard to see much through the haze of tobacco smoke. When he finally spotted a server, he motioned for another bottle of wine.

"The sooner I find myself a sensible woman, the sooner I can escape this damned round of parties and chitchat," said Matthew irritably. "What activity do you suggest next?"

Spencer drummed his fingers on the table as he thought. "Why not Covent Garden? I hear Kean is playing the lead in a particularly fine production of *Macbeth*. I wouldn't mind seeing it myself."

Matthew grimaced. "If I must, I must. I believe Lady Clarissa mentioned a fondness for the theater.

I may rise slightly in her estimation by suggesting such an expedition."

"So it is important that Lady Clarissa hold you in high esteem?"

Matthew glared at his friend. "Blast, you're as incorrigible as my uncle. No, it does not matter. It just makes life somewhat easier." He looked up with relief as the server arrived with another bottle of claret. It made a convenient break in a rather inconvenient conversation.


It was strange, thought Matthew as he watched Kean stride across the stage in a blood-drenched robe. The diminutive actor had the most irritating voice, unremarkable looks, and a somewhat odious manner. And yet, when he declaimed his lines, it was impossible to take one's eyes off him.

Clarissa obviously thought so, too, for she broke into frenzied applause as the curtain dropped for the interval.

The hum of conversation, muted but present during most of the performance, rose dramatically around them. People in boxes stood and stretched, adjusted their gloves, went off in search of refreshments.

"You seem to be enjoying the performance," Matthew remarked to Clarissa.

"It is most entertaining. And isn't Lady Macbeth astonishing? I've always loved that character. So much fortitude."

"She is a rather bloodthirsty one, though, wouldn't

you say?'' chimed in Spencer, who was sitting between Clarissa and Anne.

"She knew what she wanted and pursued it directly. I call that admirable," said Clarissa.

"Somehow, that does not surprise me," Matthew replied with an odd half-smile.

"It has been a long time since last we met, Spencer," said an unfamiliar voice from the door leading into the private box Matthew had engaged for the evening.

All four turned curiously to see their visitor. "Well, I'll be damned," cried Spencer. "Sherrington!"

" 'Tis I, indeed, fresh back from Greece and eager to see the latest thespian wonder to tread the boards. Can't say I think much of Kean, but Shakespeare, as always, is music to my ears."

Throughout this exchange, Clarissa had gazed dumbfounded at the visitor. His striking red hair stood out in vivid contrast to the hunter green cape and tapestry waistcoat that he wore. In his hand he carried an ebony walking stick with an elaborately jeweled head shaped like an Egyptian mummy. She was fascinated.

Spencer introduced him as Mr. Piers Sherrington. Clarissa gasped when she heard the name. Of course! She should have realized who he was when he mentioned Greece.

The youngest son of an esteemed family, he had left England at the tender age of sixteen to seek his muse abroad. In the process, he had become one of England's best young poets. How often Clarissa and Anne had read his epic "Rosamunde" aloud together, and had thrilled at the tragic tale of the scorned lover who drowned herself in a quiet pond! Clarissa glanced eagerly at Anne, who seemed similarly stunned to meet the famous poet in the flesh.

"Denham?" Piers mused, as he was introduced to Clarissa. "Are you, by any chance, the daughter of the Marquess of Wickford?"

"The very same. I am honored to meet you, Mr. Sherrington. I am a longtime lover of your poetry."

"A longtime lover?" he enquired slyly. "One has to appreciate that, Lady Clarissa." Coolly, he lifted her gloved hand to his lips, turned it over, and pressed a kiss to her wrist. Clarissa shivered through the thin fabric.

"What brings you back to England after so many years abroad?" she enquired somewhat shakily.

"A desire, my lady, to see again the fair shores of Albion and my dear friends here. While the Alps made my spirit soar, and Italy my heart ache, and Greece my mind play tricks, it is only in England where I feel truly at ease."

"I love to read about such places, but unfortunately I am very prone to seasickness and have never cared much for travel," Clarissa remarked.

"Perhaps we might meet again to discuss foreign climes and literary pursuits?" he enquired.

"I would enjoy that immensely."

From the corner of her eye, she saw Matthew's brows draw together in an angry frown. Probably jealous to see someone with so much more charm than himself, she thought with a small measure of malice.

"Why don't you sit with us for the rest of the performance?" asked Spencer. "There's plenty of room."

"Thank you, old friend, but I really must return to my own box. I'm with my aged grandmother, whom I haven't seen in many years, and she would be sorely offended if I left her to enjoy the rest of the performance alone. I shall take my leave for now, but I am sure we will encounter each other again soon. After all, the *ton* is a rather small and confining world, isn't it?" With a throaty laugh, he bid them *adieu* and disappeared.

"Wherever did you meet young Sherrington?" Matthew enquired blandly.

"His brother and I were acquaintances at Harrow, and I met him during a holiday I spent at their home. I've not seen him for years. I'm surprised he remembered me, to tell you the truth. I heard several weeks ago that he was back in England, but had not set eyes on him until this minute."

"He certainly seems to be pleased with himself and his travels." Matthew's forehead was still furrowed in an unbecoming frown.

"And so would you be if you were one of England's most inventive young poets," cried Clarissa with spirit.

"England's? I can't say as England can lay much claim on a man who hasn't set foot on her 'fair shores' for some ten years."

Clarissa's scathing retort was cut off as the curtain rose again for the conclusion of the play.

\* \* \*

Clarissa was playing the piano in the music room when Shaftoe appeared noiselessly at her side.

"There's a young gentleman here to see you. Mr. Piers Sherrington. I have seated him in the blue salon with Lady Lucinda and one of the maids."

Clarissa's heart made a curious little jump as she rose from the stool and tried to walk slowly from the room.

Piers rose gracefully as she entered the blue salon. She noticed that his attire was even more colorful than that of the night before. To fawn pantaloons, he had added an emerald waistcoat and a bright blue cutaway coat. The edge of a quizzing glass sparkled from his breast pocket.

"Charmed to meet again so soon, my lady," he said, as he raised her hand briefly to his lips and smiled into her eyes.

Behind him, Clarissa noticed, her young sister grimaced.

Piers, it transpired, wished to take her for a drive in Hyde Park. His barouche and coachman were waiting outside.

"A coachman?" she enquired.

"Oh yes, of course," he replied absently. "Never acquired much of a taste for horsemanship. Rather hard on one's hands. Makes it difficult to hold a pen for hours on end, as I must in pursuit of my art."

Lucy let out a long and rather gusty sigh. Clarissa shot her a scathing look.

"And you, my dear, how did you enjoy the performance last night? I never did get a chance to ask."

"I thought it was marvelous. I'm amazed you did not care for Kean. I find him a master."

"Well, he certainly can perform, I will grant him that. But such an odious little man! Really, he looks rather as if he'd be more at home in the East End than the West."

"And appearances, I suppose, are of preeminent importance for an artist?" Lucy asked with an edge of sarcasm.

Her tone was lost on the poet. "We artists are in the business of entertainment, and it behooves us to be decorative as well as useful," he replied.

Soon, Clarissa and Piers left for an enjoyable trip around the park, punctuated by many stops, as Piers leaned out of the barouche to greet a vast number of long-lost friends. Clarissa was astonished to see how many acquaintances the young man had made before leaving England so long ago, when he was hardly grown.

"Good afternoon, your grace. I was so sorry I could not be present at your ball the other evening," he called out to the Duchess of Landsborough as she passed by in an elegant curricle.

She commanded her husband to rein in the horses. "Well, Mr. Sherrington! What an astonishing surprise! I had heard you were in town. Welcome home." Suddenly, her eyes focused on Clarissa, sitting beside Piers. "And Lady Clarissa! My, you do seem to be attracting all the most eligible young men these days," she remarked.

"Ah, your grace, I just cannot resist a drive in the park," she answered airily, although she was seething with embarrassment inside. What if Mr. Sherrington thought her a shameless flirt?

The poet, however, appeared not to think less of her. "I am proud you have accepted my offer of a drive, when it appears you have many ardent swains from which to choose. I only hope the experience has been worthy of your valuable time," he said humbly.

She assured him it had, reflecting that it was pleasant to have her time and attentions considered valuable, for a change. Lord Langdon had always acted as though she owed it to him to be at his beck and call.

As they left the park, Piers leaned back against the tufted cushions of his well-appointed barouche. "Just collected this vehicle yesterday," he told her proudly. "The best there is to be had."

"It is certainly very comfortable," she informed him. It was different, though, to be riding in a covered space after the breezy freedom of Lord Langdon's curricle, she reflected. But then again, she reminded herself, to get a ride in Lord Langdon's curricle, one had to take Lord Langdon as well. All in all, it struck her that Mr. Sherrington's barouche was a much better bargain.

After a turn about the park, the barouche headed back towards Clarissa's home. Mr. Sherrington attentively helped her down from the carriage, and retained her hand. "Much too pretty a hand to be covered, no matter how fine the fabric," Piers mused. Lightly, deliberately, he tugged at Clarissa's silk glove until it came free. Again, as he had done in the theater the evening before, he turned her hand over. But this time, he placed a warm, lingering kiss on her upturned palm.

Clarissa gazed at him dumbly as he gave her back her glove. "Until we meet again, *ma chère,*" he said, as he climbed back into the carriage and motioned the coachman to proceed.

In a daze, unsure exactly what had happened, Clarissa entered the house and retired to her room. Within minutes, there was a scratch at the door and Lucy entered.

"You do seem to attract the most unattractive men," she began without preamble as she took up her favorite position, sitting on her sister's bed.

Clarissa looked at her sibling in genuine surprise. "What do you mean?"

"Oh heavens, Clarissa, doesn't he make your skin crawl? All that talk of his 'art' and his delicate hands. I think he's the most unbearable fop."

"How can you say such things about a man who writes such exquisite poetry?" And who gives such exquisite kisses, she added in her mind.

"Bah," said Lucy succinctly. "I've read that Milton himself was a horror to live with, and they say that brilliant German composer . . . you know, the one who is deaf . . . is a wretched tyrant."

"Well, Mr. Sherrington is neither a horror nor a tyrant," said Clarissa. "He's a perfect gentleman."

"I do not trust him," said Lucy solemnly.

Clarissa glanced at her in surprise. Her sister had a good sense of people, but was seldom serious and subdued enough to give it full reign. "Why do you say that?"

"I am not sure. Just a premonition." The younger girl's face was taut with worry.

Clarissa laughed gaily. "Until we have more evidence than that, I will treat him as honorable. At least he knows how to be entertaining and civil, unlike another gentleman I could mention."

Lucy, sensing she was making no progress, wisely held her tongue.

# EIGHT

"I say, that is quite the most attractive walking stick I've seen since I returned to this dreary island."

Piers was transfixed before the tiny Bond Street window of Lambeth and Howe. Clarissa followed his gaze with mild interest. Her maid, Betty, trailed behind them.

"It reminds me of those sold in a sensational shop in Vienna, where each item is carefully made by an eighty-year-old craftsman over a period of weeks," said Piers enthusiastically. "They are quite valuable, and possessing such an article makes one quite the envy of society."

"You have been to Vienna?" Clarissa asked with interest, more fascinated by the fabled city itself than by its fancy shops. "Was it as elegant as everyone claims? Did you have a chance to attend any of the sessions of the congress?"

"The congress?" Piers responded vaguely, his attention still captured by the walking stick. "Oh, yes, that political gathering. No, I am afraid such events do not interest me in the slightest. It is the life of the mind that attracts my fascination."

"Yes, of course," Clarissa replied. But Piers did not

hear her, as he had just disappeared into the minuscule shop. Reluctantly, she made to follow him when a voice cried out, "Lady Clarissa!"

She turned to see Lord Langdon's elegant curricle draw up to the pavement. The earl hopped down and bowed. "What a pleasant surprise to see you on Bond Street, my lady," he commented dryly. "I did not think you cared for shopping."

"I really do not, my lord, but I am on an outing with a friend. What brings you here?"

"I am on my way to an afternoon of dissolute revelry with Willoughby."

"Please give him my regards," said Clarissa. She had taken a strong liking to Langdon's blond friend.

As for Langdon himself, she had been amused by his attempts to enjoy their evening at the theater. His composed veneer, she suspected, had almost successfully hidden a boredom of outrageous proportions. Perhaps he, not Kean, should be taking a turn on the boards. At that thought, she chuckled.

"What amuses you, my lady?" he asked curiously.

"Nothing of importance, Matthew. I just had a vision of you as a stage actor, and I found it most entertaining."

"A stage actor?" he repeated. "Truly, I cannot think of anything more unlikely! Unless it were the role of a love-struck suitor, of course."

"Of course," she said mildly.

"My uncle is determined I should play such a role, however. I called upon you just minutes ago, only to be informed by the ever-cheerful Shaftoe that you were not at home. I wished to ask you if you and your father would favor my uncle and myself with a visit tomorrow night for dinner. He is most anxious to meet you."

Another entire night in Langdon's company! Clarissa shuddered inwardly. But it was against her nature to deny a request from one of her elders, especially an invalid. Showing the older gentleman some kindness surely would not be so difficult.

"I would be pleased, my lord."

Just then, Piers emerged from the shop, brandishing the coveted walking stick. "Why did you not accompany me into the shop, Lady Clarissa? Truly, it is a most fascinating place." Spotting Matthew, he inclined his head. "Good day, my lord."

Matthew's eyes hardened as they fastened on the dandified poet, but he returned the younger man's greeting. "Are you enjoying your explorations of London's fine shops?"

"Oh, certainly. Of course, they do not compare to the elegant establishments I frequented while abroad, but one must make do. There is nothing I love above the quest for the perfect ensemble."

Matthew shot Clarissa a wry glance, which she avoided by turning her eyes up the street. Perhaps Piers was a fop. But at least he made an attempt to be witty and entertaining. He did not constantly assail her with barbs. And his romantic nature was as evident in his manner toward her as it was in his famous odes. Matthew, with his unpolished manners and cold, practical nature, had no right to look down his aquiline nose at Piers.

"It is well that gentlemen such as you can entertain

yourselves and buoy up the British economy at the same time," Langdon commented with deceptive mildness.

"Isn't it just?" replied Piers.

"I, however, must take my leave. I am scheduled to meet a friend."

"He has a very important appointment to pursue matters of state," Clarissa inserted slyly. "An investigation of the properties of the grape and the green baize, I believe."

"Good day," said Matthew stiffly, with a withering glance at Clarissa. "Enjoy your outing." With that, he jumped lightly into his curricle, cracked the reins more energetically than was necessary, and disappeared down Bond Street.

Even in the depths of her annoyance at his overbearing ways, Clarissa could not help but admire the way Langdon handled his horses.


Spencer Willoughby was seated at his usual table when Matthew arrived in high bad humor.

"What exactly do you know about this Sherrington?" Langdon asked without preamble as he sat down and poured himself a crystal goblet of wine from the generously proportioned decanter.

"Good afternoon to you, too, Matt," his friend said with a laugh. "Why the sudden interest in England's reigning poetic genius?"

"I encountered him with Lady Clarissa a few moments ago. I find him most annoying, and I wonder if he is suitable company for a young lady."

"Lady Clarissa, I hasten to point out, is hardly a young miss fresh out of the schoolroom. I would not be at all surprised to find she is perfectly capable of choosing her own acquaintances."

Matthew glowered at the blond man across the table. "I did not mean to imply that she is foolish, although I do believe she is somewhat buffleheaded when it comes to matters romantic. I just have an uneasy feeling about his motives in pursuing her company."

Spencer pondered for a moment. "Well, I do know he came back to England fleeing his creditors in Italy. Piers always did have a fondness for fine things, but his family has never been particularly wealthy. Great land holdings, of course, but not a lot of ready blunt. But surely you don't suspect him of being a fortune hunter? For that sort of activity, there are far more well-dowered young ladies than Lady Clarissa."

"I don't know what I suspect," muttered Matthew darkly. "The man just puts my teeth on edge. And I don't think it's wise for Lady Clarissa to be seen so much in his company. A man who has spent so long abroad could have any sort of reputation."

"Reputation? Don't tell me you've become a moralist in your old age!"

"Not a moralist. Just suspicious."

A sort of suspicion that had never been particularly evident before Matt met Lady Clarissa, Spencer noted silently.

* * *

Later that afternoon, Matthew found himself back on Bond Street, in the establishment of Lambeth and Howe.

"Yes, the gentleman you describe visited today," said Mr. Howe, a short, perspiring man whose florid face was wreathed in smiles. "We were very honored, of course, to have such a famous man patronize our shop. We are but newly established on Bond Street, and most anxious to build up the right sort of clientele."

"And did this gentleman pay in coin for his trifle?"

Mr. Howe's eyes widened. "Of course not, my lord! You should know I would never insist on such a thing. All of our best customers deal strictly on credit. Mr. Sherrington being such an esteemed personage, we established an account for him immediately." He paused in thought. "A man such as yourself should examine our merchandise as well. You will find it is all of the highest quality, as befits a man of your stature."

"Perhaps another time," said Langdon brusquely.

After thanking the proprietor, he emerged onto the street, stroking his chin thoughtfully. While it was true that most of the *haute ton* relied on credit, it bothered Matthew that Sherrington had made his purchase at a store he did not normally frequent.

Matthew reclaimed his curricle and guided the horses through the late afternoon traffic. He drove through the elegant streets of Mayfair and the busy thoroughfares of the City, crowded with clerks scurrying about on the business of wealthy citizens. He continued until the rows of elegant town houses and gas lamps gave way to smaller, sootier dwellings and dim, dusty shops. Soon the streets became too narrow for his curricle. With a tug on the reins, he brought the horses to a halt.

Immediately, a small boy aged about seven appeared at the carriage's side. "Need someone to watch the rig, guv'nor?" he chirped, tugging on his rather greasy forelock.

Matthew examined the child, noting his threadbare shirt and thin face. "And what would such a service cost me?" he asked with a smile.

The boy tipped his head to one side, considering. "A shilling," he finally said decisively.

Matthew hooted with laughter. "You are an ambitious young fellow! But I admire ambition, and believe it should be rewarded."

The child looked at him uncertainly.

Matthew reached into his purse and pulled out a shining silver crown. "If you keep my curricle and horses safe, you may have this piece as a token of my gratitude."

With eyes like saucers, the urchin looked up at his benefactor. "Don't you worry, guv'nor. I knows everybody on these streets. I won't be letting anything happen."

With another smile, Matthew tossed his reins to the lad and disappeared into a dark side alley lined with pawnshops. He stopped at a tiny window rimmed with grime. Displayed inside was a haphazard collection of ancient watches, chipped snuff boxes, a moth-eaten lion's head, several women's necklaces, and an amateurish miniature in a gilded frame. The small sign above the door read Jones and Sons, Pawnbrokers.

Ducking his head, Matthew paused for a moment in the doorway to allow his eyes to adjust to the gloom inside. As he attempted to focus, he heard a nasal voice call out in greeting, "Be with you in a minute, sir!"

Presently, a spindly man of indeterminate age emerged from a door at the back of the shop, bringing with him the unmistakable odors of fried bacon and tobacco smoke. "I am Mr. Jones, the proprietor. How may I be of service to you, sir?" inquired the man, touching his forelock. "Have you something of value you wish to part with? A family heirloom, perhaps? Some jewelry, sporting equipment, or maybe a rare book?"

The man's open greed repulsed him, but Matthew forced himself to smile. "Good afternoon. I am the Earl of Langdon, and actually, I have come simply to make a few inquiries."

"Ah, you want to find out if it is worth your while before transporting your valuable belongings here. I can assure you, my lord, that I give a fair rate for everything I accept."

"I do not wish to pawn anything at all," Matthew said with irritation.

"Do you wish to make a purchase?" asked the spindly man doubtfully, as he leaned his tall frame against a rickety oak shelf.

"No, as I already said, I wish to make some inquiries. I would like to know if a certain gentleman has ever pawned anything through this establishment." Briefly, Matthew described Piers Sherrington.

"He may have been here, my lord, quite possibly. We have so many patrons," he said confidingly. "I don't know if I could recall him particularly. And, of course, many of my customers don't want that fact widely known, eh? You can understand that, of course."

Matthew sensed some additional incentive was called for. Grimacing, he withdrew the ornate pin he wore in his cravat. He had never particularly liked the ormolu piece—it had been given him as a gift. How fortunate that he had worn it today.

Placing the pin on the counter, he looked Jones squarely in the eye. "I might consider pawning this piece," he said thoughtfully. "It is not one of my favorites."

The lean man's eyes gleamed. "What sort of loan would you want for it, my lord?"

"It is yours for the price of the information I seek."

"The man in question was in here just a few days ago," Jones replied promptly. "I remember him distinctly, so I do. Brought in a cartload of things. Good quality, too." His eyes scanned the badly lit interior. "Like this, for instance." He retrieved a gold card case from a shelf behind the counter.

Matthew examined it closely. On the cover, surrounded by ornate etchings of flowers and birds, were the initials P.S.

"He said he would return once a week to pawn yet more," Jones explained eagerly. "I was quite pleased, as you can understand."

"Yes," said Matthew grimly. "Thank you for your assistance."

In several other nearby pawn shops, the story was the same. The shopkeepers all remembered the elegant red-haired man, as each had acquired quite a bit of booty from him.

Sighing heavily, Matthew retraced his steps and retrieved his carriage, tossing his young helper the crown as he vaulted into his seat.

"Good luck to ye, guv'nor," the child cried as Matthew moved the carriage away from the pavement.

It was Sherrington who would need good luck, Matthew reflected, if he made any attempt to pull Clarissa into his spendthrift net.

# NINE

Dabbing her lips with a fine white linen napkin, Clarissa glanced across the table at her host. "You have a most skilled cook," she said. "It was a thoroughly enjoyable repast."

"Thank you, my dear," replied Walter Carstairs with a warm smile. "I hope you will return to visit us often," he added, with a speaking look at Matthew, who glowered in return.

It had not been the most relaxed meal she had ever attended, Clarissa reflected, although Matthew's uncle was exceedingly charming and even Matthew himself had been on his best behavior. But there was an underlying tension in the earl's manner that Clarissa was at a loss to understand.

"I have been so absorbed in your delightful conversation that I completely neglected to ask after your father. We were once acquaintances, many years ago. I hope his illness tonight is not serious?" Walter Carstairs asked.

"Oh no, it is just his gout. It bothers him occasionally, but he has learned to cope. He was truly sorry he could not be here tonight," replied Clarissa. Despite his illness, her father had insisted she attend the dinner without him, laughing off her protests that it would be unseemly for her to attend alone. "We are almost family, after all," he had chuckled. Since her "courtship" with Lord Langdon had commenced, her father had been the soul of joviality. She was dreading the day when Matthew cried off. Unlike the earl, she was becoming less certain that her father would accept the news with equanimity.

"And your mother? I once spent an extremely enjoyable evening at one of her salons."

Matthew looked at his uncle with surprise, and Clarissa regarded him with gratitude. Most new acquaintances avoided mentioning Lady Wickford altogether, feeling any discussion of Clarissa's mother would draw embarrassing attention to the Wickfords' unusual living arrangements.

"My mother is quite well, thank you. I visited with her just the other day."

"She is a wonderfully lively woman. She reminds me a great deal of my own dear Mary," Walter Carstairs replied, a fond light brightening his eyes.

Matthew suddenly jumped into the conversation. "Perhaps, since we are all finished our meal, we might repair to the drawing room for tea?"

When his uncle nodded his agreement, Matthew rose from his chair and offered the older gentleman his arm. Slowly, Walter rose from his elegantly upholstered chair, gripping his nephew's arm firmly. Carefully, Matthew guided him away from the table.

"Don't worry about me, for goodness' sake. You should be squiring Lady Clarissa about," the older man grumbled. Nonetheless, he leaned heavily on his strongly built nephew.

"I am sure Lady Clarissa will understand my momentary lapse in manners, Uncle. She is a rather independent young woman, and I do not doubt she is capable of finding her way to our drawing room unassisted." He turned back to smile over his relative's bowed head.

Clarissa smiled back in return, more in reaction to Matthew's manner toward his uncle than in response to his quip. Following the slow-moving pair, she reflected that Matthew had shown a completely different side of himself this evening than he had previously displayed to her. While tense, he had been unfailingly polite and considerate to his uncle. He had urged the older man to eat more vegetables, asked the footman to open a window when his uncle became slightly flushed, and kept up a steady stream of light, amusing conversation.

As Matthew swung open the double doors of the drawing room, Clarissa could not restrain a quiet gasp of pleasure.

"It is a marvelous room, isn't it?" asked Walter Carstairs delightedly as Matthew helped him settle into a large wing chair near the roaring fire, and pulled a rug up over his knees. "It has always been one of my favorites."

"Marvellous does not begin to describe it." Clarissa had been impressed by the stately elegance of the quiet parlor where they had met before dinner, but the drawing room was opulent beyond her wildest imaginings. She had attended balls and routs in many of London's finest residences, but never in her experience had she seen a room such as this.

Decorated in the palest shades of yellow and green, highlighted with intricate white plasterwork, the room seemed to glow with a life of its own. All the furnishings, Clarissa noted with astonishment, had been specially created to match the decor. Pale green, marble-topped tables, supported by deceptively delicate-looking legs, held books of prints and poetry. A fitted green-and-yellow carpet repeated the mythical motifs of the plasterwork. Even the china doorknobs had been made in the exact shades of the walls and carpet. An enormous pier glass, topped with two plasterwork gryphons, stood between two gleaming windows, which Clarissa supposed faced onto the small garden. The room's crowning glory was the elaborate ceiling, festooned with plasterwork and studded with small, vibrantly hued paintings of classical scenes.

One might think such a room would be overwhelming, Clarissa thought, but the coordinated elements combined to give the chamber an aura of peace and serenity.

"One could live quite happily in such a room for all of one's life," she said finally, after a period of stunned silence.

On either side of the enormous chimneypiece hung two compelling portraits. One was a richly colored, life-sized painting of a young woman with reddish curls and a sweet, pensive face. On her lap she held what appeared to be a very contented cat. From her gown, Clarissa guessed that the portrait dated from about the same time as the room's appointments, about thirty years previously.

Walter Carstairs noticed her admiration of the painting. "That is a portrait of my dear Mary," he said proudly. "That cat was her constant companion."

"She is very beautiful," said Clarissa warmly.

"The other portrait depicts young Matthew's mother," continued the older gentleman, directing Clarissa's gaze to a painting of a young woman with rich chestnut hair. She stood before a pastoral scene of summer trees and shepherds, and gazed confidently out of the frame. "Is not her smile appealing?" asked Walter Carstairs. "She was always smiling."

"It lights up her whole face," said Clarissa, immediately struck by the family resemblance. "I can see where the earl takes after her."

Matthew gave a surprised start at that comment. "Do you, really? I have never seen the likeness, myself."

"Perhaps that is because you smile so seldom, my lord."

"Yes, he has become a somewhat crotchety creature of late, hasn't he?" said Matthew's uncle, oblivious to the underlying tension in the room. "I must say, I admire you for putting up with his grumbling ways."

Just then, the housekeeper arrived with a silver tea tray loaded with delicate cups and saucers. Clarissa took the task of pouring for the gentlemen. They chatted on about inconsequential topics. Then, after Clarissa and Matthew had been embroiled in a lengthy discussion of London's gardens for some minutes, they heard a gentle snore.

Matthew grinned. "It's not the company, I assure you. My uncle will be most chagrined when he discovers he has dropped off again."

"Oh, no offense taken, my lord. I think he has done admirably well this evening. I could tell from the rings around his eyes that he was not feeling particularly well."

Matthew glanced at her curiously.

"My grandmother had consumption when I was a young child. I recognize the signs," Clarissa explained.

"Well, then, you understand the situation. I am grateful," said Matthew awkwardly.

"Perhaps I should take my leave now, and allow your uncle time to rest." Clarissa rose from her chair.

"No, please, wait." The urgency in Lord Langdon's tone surprised Clarissa, and she reseated herself with reluctance. "There is something I wish to discuss with you, but I did not wish to bring it up in front of my uncle."

Matthew paused, then sighed. "I am sure you will react adversely to this advice, but I feel it necessary to warn you against keeping company with Mr. Sherrington," he began stiffly.

"Whatever for?" cried Clarissa in surprise. "He is a well-born gentleman, with fame and charm in addition." She paused, considering. "Surely you are not restricting my accessibility to other gentlemen simply because I am acting as your tutor?"

"Of course not!" Matthew exclaimed. "You can dally at routs and revels every evening with a string of young gentlemen on your arm, if you so wish. It is no affair of mine. But I am concerned about Mr. Sherrington's motives in seeking out your company."

"Perhaps he simply enjoys being with me," Clarissa shot back with equal heat. "Surely that is not so hard to fathom?"

Matthew sighed and ran his fingers through his dark curls distractedly. "I see I am not making a very good job of this. My apologies. Let me cut right to the quick. I am very much afraid that Mr. Sherrington is a fortune hunter."

"Now you are being completely ridiculous!" Clarissa exclaimed. "If he is a fortune hunter, why on earth would he seek me as a likely source of funds? As you yourself have not shied from observing, my family circumstances are by no means substantial." Scorn dripped from Clarissa's words.

"I suspect that our fine poet is unaware of that fact. It has been many years since he lived in England, and he may not be aware of the recent misfortunes that have befallen your father."

"What has led you to these extraordinary conclusions?" Clarissa sat rigidly in her chair and stared at Matthew. Of all the unmitigated gall! she thought.

"Spence mentioned to me this afternoon that young Sherrington had fled the Continent to escape some particularly avid creditors. I did a bit of investigation, and discovered that he has been frequenting the pawnshops of Spitalfields, distributing cartloads of his personal possessions."

"So he wishes to dispense with some unfashionable items. You yourself must have noticed that he always dresses in the very latest style. Would it not make sense to recoup some of his investment?"

"Perhaps, but then why does he favor only new shops in his quest for the latest fashion? I suspect it is because all the established firms have denied him credit."

"Really, my lord, you are an embittered and cynical man. Just because someone enjoys life, and enjoys my company, you suspect sinister motives."

"I am only acting in your best interests."

"I would thank you, my lord, to leave my interests to me. Our arrangement does not extend to your interference in my personal affairs." Clarissa paused, then continued with vigor. "Perhaps it is time for us to end this little charade. I think you have learned just about as much as I feel like teaching you."

"And what will your father say?" Matthew jeered.

"When you meet with him to tell him you wish to withdraw your suit, I believe he will be satisfied."

"And if I do not?"

Clarissa stared at him, confused. "I cannot imagine why you would wish to continue to see me. As you have demonstrated, you obviously think I am a cloth-headed fool who cannot see for herself when she is being exploited."

"In this matter, and this matter only, I do happen to think you are being a cloth-headed fool," Matthew retorted. "It perplexes me to see a woman of your demonstrated intelligence out on the town with that foppish twit. What is it about him, exactly, that has so fascinated your interest?"

"For one thing, he is all the things you are not: amusing, congenial, romantic . . ."

"Ah, yes, romance. How could I forget how highly you rate hearts and flowers?" said Matthew acidly. "Is it his high-flown odes that have you so enthralled? Or perhaps he has treated you to a brief kiss which has spun your maidenly head?"

Clarissa could feel her cheeks flush, and yet again cursed her fair skin.

Matthew must have noticed the blush, too, for he continued in a dangerous tone, "Ah, I see the damsel can be swayed by mere physical passion. If it is that you seek, you would have been wise to accept my suit after all. I may not know or care for the intricacies of courting, but I assure you that I do know how to kiss."

Rising from his chair, he strode towards Clarissa and with one swift move lifted her from her seat. She shot a warning look toward the chair on the other side of the fire where Walter Carstairs sat contentedly snoring, but Matthew ignored her apprehension.

"Just remember that anyone can be a skilled seducer," he murmured intently. "One does not have to be 'in love' to give an accomplished performance." With that, he bent his head swiftly to hers.

Gasping in astonishment and fury, Clarissa had no time to protest before Matthew's lips came down on hers. Her mind reeling, her first reaction was to struggle. But her curiosity and her body's peculiar reactions overcame her better judgement, and she allowed him to continue.

With one of his arms braced strongly against her back, his hand cradling her head so that she could not move it away, Matthew slowly moved his other hand up the light bodice of her dress. Clarissa, barely aware of his actions, drew in her breath sharply when his hand brushed lightly against her breast, then came to rest there. Despite herself, she shuddered with pleasure.

Unthinkingly, she cast her arms around his neck. His lips became more insistent on her own. Instinctively, she parted her lips and shivered as his tongue explored her mouth.

They stayed in that position for some moments. Clarissa felt dizzy, and her legs threatened to give way beneath her.

Abruptly, Lord Langdon broke off the kiss and pushed her away from him. "As I said, it takes no particular feeling to act the part of a skilled seducer," he said, as he observed Clarissa with a clouded, unreadable expression.

"But it takes good breeding and manners to avoid acting the part of a seducer with a woman for whom one cares not," replied Clarissa raggedly, trying to regain control of her senses. "I believe our evening is at an end, Lord Langdon. If you would be so kind as to summon my carriage, I wish to return home." He did not move. "Now," she added weakly, wondering how much longer she would be able to maintain her facade of imperturbability.

Wordlessly, Matthew left the room to summon his groom. Clarissa collapsed in a nearby chair. A few moments later, it was not Matthew, but the housekeeper, who entered the room to tell Clarissa the carriage was ready.

# TEN

Really, Lord Langdon was the most impossible man. Clarissa kept her carefully hooded gaze fastened on the gentleman in question as he made his way across the floor of Almack's.

Having expressed his disinterest in courting rituals on more than one occasion, and his hatred of assembly rooms such as Almack's in particular, he was now spending an entire evening within these walls lavishing the most outrageous attentions on Miss Isabella Larkin. As Clarissa observed the couple, Langdon left not once, but twice, to retrieve cups of lemonade for the fair lady. When he spoke to Miss Larkin intently and then lifted her hand to press a gentle kiss against her fingers, Clarissa turned away with a disgusted sigh.

"Whatever is the matter, O light of my life?" cried Mr. Sherrington as he approached her carrying two plates of sweets. Handing her one, he looked at her with concern. "You are wearing the most inauspicious frown. Not at all suitable attire for a glittering assembly such as this. Not at all."

Remembering her manners, Clarissa summoned up a pleasant expression. "Please forgive me, Mr. Sherrington, I was lost in some unimportant musings. It is not the evening or the company, please rest assured."

"That pleases me greatly, my lady. Your happiness is, of course, my penultimate concern. When clouds cross your beautiful countenance, my own sun disappears."

Such flowery compliments would have turned Clarissa's head just a day or two previously. Why, then, did Mr. Sherrington's remarks leave her unmoved today? Perhaps, she reflected, she put more stock in Lord Langdon's suppositions than she had previously suspected.

Could Mr. Sherrington be a fortune hunter?

Somehow, gazing at him, she found it hard to believe. From the tip of his tall beaver hat to the toes of his shiny Hessian boots, he was flawlessly arrayed in the very latest fashion. Perhaps his sky-blue waistcoat was a bit more extravagant than those worn by other gentlemen in the assembly, but he was a creative soul, after all, and must have an outlet, she reasoned. All of his apparel was of the finest quality. Surely a man short of funds would not be so precipitate as to throw away his meager resources on something as frivolous as clothing?

Her musings were interrupted by that gentleman's clear voice. "Lady Clarissa, you are so far away. Please return to earth and join me for a spin about the dance floor. The orchestra is about to strike up a waltz. It reminds me so of my beloved Vienna, I cannot stand aside." He paused and contemplated her intently. "Your beauty is far too boundless to be confined here to the edges of the room. Please, graciously share it with the assembled company."

Clarissa, confused, gave her hand to Mr. Sherrington and allowed him to lead her on to the dance floor. Never in her life had she had such an avid and complimentary suitor. Even the two gentlemen who had offered for her during past Seasons had tempered their admiration by politely complimenting other ladies occasionally, and by circulating widely in any gathering. Mr. Sherrington's attentions verged on poor manners, as he focused his gaze solely on her, attended to her every whim, and showered her with compliments at every opportunity. Truth to tell, all this admiration made Clarissa a little uncomfortable. But certainly this was the way of things with all poets, she reasoned with herself. Consumed by passions unknown to more subdued souls—and Clarissa could not help but think of the Earl of Langdon—poets were more likely than most to step outside the bounds of propriety in their quest to pursue their goals. And wasn't that what she so admired about poets in the first place?

Uneasily, she took her place opposite Mr. Sherrington and allowed him to take her into his arms for the waltz. Many of the younger misses, Clarissa noted, had removed themselves to the gilt chairs aligned along the walls of the ballroom. Although the once-scandalous dance was now the height of fashion, now that the Prince of Wales himself had given it his approval, timid young women just out in Society were still somewhat hesitant to participate in it. Clarissa herself had no such worries, she reflected wryly. After four Seasons, she was hardly a shy, naive miss.

"Ah, my dear, you are quite simply the most ravishing woman in this room," Mr. Sherrington remarked as they began to slowly circle the dance floor.

Clarissa flushed and said nothing, but her insides were beginning to churn painfully. She knew for a fact that she was by no means a beauty. Mr. Sherrington's florid compliments, which had once seemed so pleasurable, were now like gnats chewing their way into her happiness.

"Please smile, Lady Clarissa. I cannot bear to see anyone unhappy in such a festive assembly," Mr. Sherrington urged.

"My apologies," she said absently. Gazing around the room, she observed Lord Langdon skimming across the floor with the dazzling Miss Larkin. Determined not to repeat her embarrassing stumble at the Duchess of Landsborough's ball, she tore her eyes away from the pair and began a conversation with Mr. Sherrington. Fortunately, that was not difficult, as she simply asked him how he came to write "Guinevere's Lament." His eyes lighting up with excitement, he proceeded to tell her of the creative process that had resulted in his most famous work to date.

Clarissa became caught up in the captivating rhythm of the waltz. She noted with surprise that Mr. Sherrington was but a tolerable dancer. His limited skill did not inhibit her enjoyment of the dance. However, after the first piece, he confessed himself "done in," and led her from the floor.

As they crossed to the refreshment table, she was

astonished to see Lord Langdon crossing the floor toward them quickly. As she moved to help herself to a glass of lemonade, Lord Langdon flashed her one of his most dazzling smiles.

"Not so quickly, Lady Clarissa. If I may, I would like to claim you for the next dance."

Clarissa observed him suspiciously. "Why, Lord Langdon," she exclaimed with feigned innocence. "I did not realize you were such an enthusiastic dancer. You have just completed several energetic sets with Miss Larkin."

"And that, Lady Clarissa, is precisely the reason I wish to dance the next set with you. One must never spend too long in the company of one individual," he noted wryly with a pointed glance at Mr. Sherrington. "Such an action could lead to unseemly gossip."

With a word to Mr. Sherrington, Clarissa capitulated to Lord Langdon's request and returned to the floor. As he swung her lightly in his arms, she tried to avoid unseemly comparisons between his effortless style and the labored pace of Mr. Sherrington. She almost succeeded.

"You are looking very lovely tonight, Lady Clarissa." Matthew's smooth baritone cut into her thoughts. "That color of silk brings out your eyes marvelously."

"Thank you, my lord," she said with surprise, remembering their recent harsh words. Perhaps he had decided to put their disagreement behind them. If he was prepared to be civil, she could certainly do the same. "I do find this gown rather warm, unfortunately. I had forgotten what a crush Almack's is. Perhaps a muslin would have been more apropos."

"Ah, the trials one must bear to be decorative," said Langdon with a chuckle. "We gentlemen do not face such difficulties."

"I do not mind so much. And, on the contrary, I feel sympathy for you gentlemen. Those neckcloths must be highly uncomfortable in such warm weather."

"It is bearable. Once, shortly after I entered Oxford, one of the seniors asked me to run to the village to collect his new frock coat and boots from the tailor. He was insistent that I make it to the village and back within the hour, as he needed the outfit for some assembly that evening. It was an extremely warm day for April, and I was decked out in the full school regalia. Wool, of course. But refusing a request from a senior student was tantamount to social suicide at Magdalen. So I sprinted to town, collected the articles, returned with five minutes to spare . . . and promptly collapsed outside the infirmary. That," he concluded with a grin, "was miserable. The present discomfort is quite tolerable."

"How terrible!" said Clarissa. "I have often wished that I could attend university, but after hearing such a tale I am just as satisfied to expand my education at home through books from the circulating library."

"It was not so horrible as you perceive. The senior student was impressed that I had finished the task. He is now a junior minister in Lord Liverpool's cabinet. Perhaps I will be able to call on that respect some day."

"You, my lord, are a born politician."

"And you, my lady, are an astute judge of character."

They shared a laugh as they twirled around the dance floor.

"Are you still laboring to promote the poor-law reform?" Clarissa asked.

"It is slow work, but I believe we are making progress. Lord Stowcroft, while still disapproving, makes his comments within the bounds of civility."

"That is indeed an achievement, my lord. I have rarely known Lord Stowcroft to maintain a facade of decorum with any regularity."

Lord Langdon chuckled. "As for the rest of our opponents, they are beginning to come around. The recent riots have unsettled even the most conservative of them, and they are beginning to see the wisdom of adopting relief measures before full-scale insurrection breaks out. Even Lord Farcastle has come round, as his tenants in particular have been suffering since the poor harvest last fall."

"Has the Chancellor of the Exchequer indicated that he will make funds available for such a purpose? I remember reading in the *Quarterly Review* . . ." Clarissa stopped. In the middle of this fascinating conversation, she did not want to encourage Lord Langdon's disapproval of her unfeminine pursuits.

Lord Langdon, however, responded to her question directly. "Yes, he agrees with us that the funds would be better spent now than later. I anticipate that he will authorize at least moderate expenditures soon. My uncle and I were discussing this very issue just this afternoon." He paused. "Uncle was quite taken with you, Lady Clarissa. He enjoyed our dinner together immensely."

"As did I," Clarissa said demurely, but her face flamed as she remembered Lord Langdon's lips on hers at the close of that evening. Perhaps sensing her discomfort, her partner switched the topic. Unfortunately, the subject he selected only added to her discomfort.

"I see Mr. Sherrington is paying you even more concentrated attention than is his usual wont," Lord Langdon observed. "I hope you are bearing my advice in mind and are treating him with caution."

Clarissa's heart sank. She should have known better than to expect Lord Langdon to be gregarious for an entire dance. "Since you have nothing on which to base your accusations but some chance bits of information, I have taken your advice with the seriousness it demanded," she replied sharply. A bit too sharply, perhaps. Clarissa was reluctant to admit, even to herself, how deeply Lord Langdon's suspicions had taken root in her own soul.

Her partner's eyes narrowed. "I think, perhaps, the lady doth protest too much."

"I think, perhaps, that the gentleman is twisting Shakespeare's words into meanings he did not intend." She paused, and her gaze fell on Miss Larkin, turning around the floor with a dashing young member of the Horse Guards. "I see that, while you are wasting time on an incorrigible cloth-head like myself, Miss Larkin has found amusing company."

"Unlike Mr. Sherrington, I do not seek to gain an iron hold on any lady's time and affections."

"Oh, never let it be said that you wished to gain any lady's affections," said Clarissa acidly. "I know, for you have told me, that such a goal is beneath your lofty ambitions."

"Miss Larkin seems to understand, as I do, that any alliance in a society such as ours must, of necessity, be based on logical foundations," he said. "While she is undoubtedly beautiful, her father is but a baron. Naturally, she wishes to use her . . . talents to move to the forefront of society. An alliance with a gentleman of higher station is a very understandable goal."

"What of love, and understanding, and mutual respect? Are they not understandable goals, as well?"

"Understandable, I suppose, but often unattainable. I do not fault you for your idealism, Lady Clarissa. I merely seek to temper it with a clear picture of the world as it is."

"Ah, so now it is you giving me lessons in the ways of society," hissed Clarissa furiously. "I am much obliged to you for your proffered assistance, my lord, but I must assure you I neither require it nor appreciate it."

"I fail to see how you will appreciate love or respect, if you do find it, if you cannot take some simple, well-meant advice graciously," said Lord Langdon coldly.

Clarissa did not deign to respond to her partner's accusation, and they finished the dance in silence.

"It looks like you and Lord Langdon were having a deep discussion out there on the floor," observed Mr. Sherrington when Clarissa joined him. "Terribly serious chap, ain't he?"

Clarissa did not reply, but merely gazed at the gentleman in question as he returned to Miss Isabella Larkin's side. Her eyes narrowed imperceptibly as he escorted the younger woman out to the terrace. Perhaps he was suffering from the heat after all, Clarissa thought wryly. But somehow, she doubted it.

"Don't you think Lady Antonia's fan is delightful?" asked Isabella Larkin. She held lightly to Lord Langdon's arm as they promenaded around the small garden.

Matthew was about to make some noncommittal comment on the accessory, which truth to tell he had not noticed, when Miss Larkin continued animatedly, "I must make an excursion to her milliner's tomorrow, for it is quite the most fascinating fan I have seen in many months. Perhaps I could commission one in green, to match my new gown. Mama says I must have a completely new ensemble for the Marchioness of Clarendon's ball, which is only a fortnight away."

Matthew nodded abstractedly, and made comments occasionally as seemed to be required of him. Isabella, for the most part, was quite content to control most of the conversation. Unfortunately, Matthew reflected, her topics of discourse rarely interested him, and he was often at a loss to make relevant observations.

Engaging conversation, he mused, might be an attractive gift in a wife, but was not strictly necessary. At least with Miss Larkin, he was not constantly on guard to parry a biting quip or impertinent question, as he was with Lady Clarissa. Conversing with Isabella, while not stimulating, was not particularly taxing, either. If they were to wed, it was unlikely that they would be required to spend long hours in conversation, at any rate. Miss Larkin greatly loved to gossip with her friends and visit the shops during the day, and in the evenings a round of social events would make the necessity of intimate conversation less pressing.

Matthew tried to observe Miss Larkin with an impartial eye. She was unmistakably beautiful, her family was of impeccable breeding and her dowry was handsome. Moreover, she harbored no romantic images about marriage. He secretly suspected her main interest in him was actually rooted in the attractions of Stonecourt. She had remarked on several occasions that she had heard much of its splendor, and that the mistress of such an establishment would be fortunate indeed.

Yes, he believed he had found the perfect woman for his businesslike marriage. He would offer for her. Soon.

# ELEVEN

Mr. Sherrington handed Clarissa up into his carriage, then moved to the opposite side to clamber in beside her somewhat awkwardly. The driver clucked to the horses, and the carriage pulled away from Almack's and moved into the dim street.

"A most enjoyable assembly, was it not, my lady?" he remarked jovially. "Such a crush of people! And I encountered several ardent admirers of my work. Really, it was most gratifying."

"Yes," Clarissa said briefly. Her head was throbbing, whether from the heat or from the unpleasantness of her encounter with Lord Langdon, she did not know. But she was anxious to reach Denham House and retire.

"It is pleasant to be back in England. My work has required me to travel extensively, of course." He paused, and cleared his throat. "The expense of voyaging abroad has been rising each year, what with the unfortunate hostilities on the Continent."

"I would imagine," said Clarissa. An uneasy voice in the back of her head wondered where this conversation was leading.

"And I recently discovered, during a most unpleasant conversation with my esteemed father, that my legacy is not as ample as I had assumed."

Warning bells rang in Clarissa's head, increasing her headache to monumental levels.

Mr. Sherrington's voice dropped to a confidential murmur. "I know you enjoy my work, as you have mentioned to me on several occasions. Have you ever, my lady, considered becoming a patron of the arts?"

Clarissa felt sick. Lord Langdon had been correct after all. Unable to look at the gentleman next to her, for whom she was beginning to feel an unbearable repugnance, she gazed out the window bleakly. "No, I have not."

Impervious to the bitterness in her voice, Mr. Sherrington continued on a note of gaiety. "Well then, my lady, allow me to be the first to offer you such an opportunity! I know that for someone in your position, a contribution of, say, five hundred pounds would not be out of line?"

Clarissa turned abruptly to face him. "Five hundred pounds! Are you mad?" In her astonishment, her well-bred manners evaporated. "I have never in my life seen five hundred pounds together in one place. Should I wish to give such an extraordinary amount to anyone, I should be completely unable. My pin money, I assure you, has never accumulated to such a total."

Piers Sherrington's eyes narrowed, and for a brief second in the dark carriage, Clarissa felt oddly afraid. But then his countenance cleared and he flashed his most charming smile. "Of course not, my dear. No woman would carry that sort of blunt in her reticule,

I understand. But surely a simple request to your papa is all that is needed to raise the necessary?"

Clarissa was now openly gaping at her companion. "I am afraid you have been misled," she told him frostily. "Contrary to your evident perception, neither I, nor my father, nor anyone in our family, has great resources. My late grandfather, probably around the time you left England ten years ago, made some rather imprudent investments in new agricultural machinery. We sustained great losses. Our estate in Kent suffered from dreadful flooding several years ago, and my father made the necessary repairs to our tenants' homes. Our financial situation hardly places us among the families who could assist you in any meaningful way," she concluded grimly, "should we wish to do so in the first place."

Mr. Sherrington made no attempt to conceal the anger now evident on his face. Even in the dim gaslight, Clarissa could see the knots forming at his throat, and the perspiration running from his forehead.

"You have misled me!" he said with feeling.

"I have misled you?" Clarissa cried with equal heat. "Have I ever given you reason to believe I was a wealthy heiress?"

"Why, your family's home . . ."

"Is mortgaged to the limit . . ."

"And that beautiful emerald ring you always wear . . ."

"Is the sole memento I have of my grandmother, and the only truly valuable piece of jewelry I own."

Mr. Sherrington, his face a deepening shade of red,

seemed to search for words. "You neglected to inform me of the fact that your family circumstances were straitened," he finally muttered, with the air of a child denied a second helping of pudding.

"If I had known that it was of such vital import to you, I would have made certain that my father showed you his books upon your first visit to Denham House. I assumed, however, that you were interested in me. I see now," she muttered in bitter fury and embarrassment, "that I was mistaken."

"Oh, my lady," said Mr. Sherrington, some of his charming manner seeping back into his voice. "Do not take it so to heart. I had assumed that, since you were somewhat more . . . mature than the other young ladies, that you were more attuned to the ways of the world. Please forgive my presumption."

There it was again—a reference to Clarissa's supposed lack of intelligence concerning the "real" world. She could have wept from frustration and embarrassment. The worst of it all was that Lord Langdon had been completely correct, and she had treated him shamefully.

"It does not matter," she said flatly. "Please, let us not mention it again."

When the carriage drew up before Denham House, Mr. Sherrington alighted, then handed Clarissa down. He gazed into her eyes intently.

"My most heartfelt apologies, my lady," he murmured. Then, as had become his custom, he pressed a warm kiss into her gloved palm. This evening, however, Clarissa felt none of the thrill that action had previously called up inside her. She felt empty and achingly alone.

"May I call upon you again soon?" Mr. Sherrington asked. "I do not wish this awkward matter to interfere with our friendship."

"As you wish," she said dully. "Good evening, Mr. Sherrington."

As she entered the foyer and gave her wrap to Shaftoe, Clarissa was surprised to see her father emerge from his study.

"I did not expect to see you up and about so late in the evening, Father."

"It is not so very late. Did you enjoy your evening with Sherrington?"

"An evening at Almack's is always diverting," she replied evasively.

"Young Sherrington has been making quite the pest of himself around here lately. Langdon had better make haste if he means to offer for you. It's not as though you are without other admirers." He regarded her fondly.

If he only knew the truth of the matter, he would probably have Betty packing her clothes within the hour for the trip to Great-Aunt Agatha's.

"I am certain that Lord Langdon will ask for an interview with you in his own time," said Clarissa in an attempt to sound demure. Her father did not need to know, just yet, exactly what Lord Langdon intended to say in that interview. Any day now, Clarissa assumed, Matthew would inform her father that he and Clarissa "did not suit."

"Sherrington may be first off the mark," Lord

Wickford countered jovially. "Can't say as I'd be as happy to see you wed to a poet as to an earl, but I know you are of a literary bent. Whatever course makes you happiest, my dear, as long as you are wed." He smiled at her indulgently.

This sudden evidence of fatherly concern, at such a late date, was more than Clarissa could bear. With a hasty goodnight to her father, she fled up the stairs to her rooms.

Lord Wickford assumed the tears in her eyes were tears of joy.


The next day, Clarissa uncharacteristically stayed in bed. Her headache of the previous evening had intensified, and her eyes felt gritty and hot.

She had informed Mrs. Harrison that she would not be at home to any visitors. Therefore, she was somewhat surprised to hear a light scratching at her door.

"Please, Mrs. Harrison, I am really not up to snuff today," she called out wearily.

"Not even to see your own sister?" came Lucy's teasing voice.

Clarissa sighed. She could hardly turn Lucy away, although the younger girl's high spirits would probably serve only to depress her further. She called out her permission for Lucy to enter.

Lucy skipped in and, in deference to her sister's pale white face and drawn expression, sat on the delicate dressing table chair instead of bouncing onto the bed. "You have been quite the popular miss today. It's unfortunate that you have taken to your bed."

"What has been happening?" asked Clarissa without interest.

"Lord High and Mighty came to call . . . twice, as a matter of fact. He seemed quite perturbed when you were not available."

"Lord Langdon was here?" Clarissa's voice was tinged with puzzlement. After their harsh words of the past few days, her termination of their "training" sessions and Lord Langdon's demonstrated interest in Miss Isabella Larkin, Clarissa had fully expected that he would cease his calls to Denham House. What could he possibly want? Perhaps he wished to inform her of his engagement to Miss Larkin. Illogically, the thought of that event made Clarissa even more despondent. She sighed.

Lucy, however, had continued to prattle along. "Anne also came by. She seemed quite determined to gain your cooperation in some matter, but she would not elaborate upon it to me." Lucy's offended look finally wrested a weak laugh from her sister.

"Do not worry about it. I am sure it is not so mysterious. Probably too complicated to explain twice over." Clarissa paused in thought. "Would you inform Mrs. Harrison that I will receive Anne if she calls again, but that I am still unavailable to anyone else—especially Lord Langdon and Mr. Sherrington."

Lucy looked at her sister with interest. "What has transpired between you, Lord High and Mighty, and Mr. Snivel?"

"Lucy! Please stop calling them by those atrocious names!" Clarissa cried, suppressing with difficulty an overwhelming urge to giggle. "I find it difficult to believe that you are to have your come-out next year. If I did not know better, I would think you were just beginning your years in the schoolroom, not ending them."

"Perhaps if people would treat me as an adult, by sharing their secrets, I would be better able to fulfil my part. As it is, everyone treats me as a mere child, so what choice do I have but to act as one?"

Lucy's indignant face finally loosed her sister's pent-up laughter.

"Well, I suppose I should be pleased that you are looking more the thing," said Lucy darkly. "But it rankles me to know that it is at my expense."

"I am sorry, dearest Lucy," said Clarissa, still chuckling. "But I do thank you. It seems as though I have had precious little to laugh about lately."

The next afternoon, Clarissa had retired to her rooms with a new Maria Edgeworth novel when Mrs. Harrison came to the door to announce Anne's arrival.

When Clarissa descended to the blue salon, her friend immediately inquired as to the state of her health. Upon hearing that it was much improved, Anne nodded and then fell uncharacteristically silent.

"Whatever is the matter?" Clarissa asked, taking a seat on the sofa. "You appear most distraught."

"I am, somewhat. I have come to ask you a favor, and I do so hope you will oblige me."

"Certainly, I will do my best. Has not each of us always come to the other's rescue?" Clarissa, for the minute, forgot her own problems, as she turned her attention to her friend's worries.

With a deep breath, Anne began her tale. "Do you remember that dreadful major who plagued me last year, and refused to listen to my pleas that my affections were already directed elsewhere?"

"Of course I remember! Who could forget Major Stokes?" Clarissa smiled at the memory of the florid-faced soldier, twice Anne's age, who had pursued her friend relentlessly with poetry and flowers.

"He has sold out his commission and returned to England permanently. He called upon me yesterday afternoon, while Mama and I were doing some embroidery, and invited me to accompany him to Vauxhall Gardens this evening. Without giving me a chance to respond, Mama leapt to accept his invitation on my behalf. As though I were some simpering young miss unable to make her own decisions," Anne huffed. "Mama always did favor the major. I did not wish to cause a scene, so I acquiesced, but I did ask the major if you could accompany us. He appeared rather crestfallen—I rather think he had anticipated an intimate *tête-à-tête*—but he agreed to my request. I simply cannot face him with only a servant for company," Anne concluded, frowning.

"Of course I will help you," said Clarissa warmly. "It will do me good to escape from my room. I have been spending far too much time alone, brooding."

"Has something untoward happened?" Anne asked, looking toward the salon's closed door. She dropped her voice. "Your father has not decided to banish you to your great-aunt's after all?"

"No, nothing so severe, although he may well do so if he ever hears of the events of last evening." She recounted the tale, coloring at the memory of her harsh words to Lord Wickford and her embarrassing carriage ride with Mr. Sherrington.

"How perfectly dreadful!" Anne breathed. "It must be all his years abroad that have given Mr. Sherrington such shameful manners."

"I have no cause to disparage shameful manners," said Clarissa bleakly. "Not when one considers how I have treated Lord Langdon, who had only my best interests at heart. If I had listened to him, I would not be in this dilemma."

"It was a lapse in judgement, to be sure, but do not torture yourself so on Lord Langdon's behalf. Remember, after all, his unseemly proposal to you. He seems to be a man upon whom emotional affairs have little impact."

Clarissa smiled at her friend. "Perhaps you are right. Onward to Vauxhall!"


If Lady Anne Beecher had happened to see Matthew Carstairs, Lord Langdon that afternoon, she might not have been so hasty in her judgement of that gentleman's equanimity.

He was sitting morosely at Spencer Willoughby's favorite table at White's, nursing a glass of port. When Willoughby himself appeared, Lord Langdon glowered at the blond man and motioned him into a chair.

"Thought you would never get here," Matthew muttered.

"Didn't realize you were waiting on me. There are some days I don't venture into White's at all, believe it or not," said his friend with a smile. "Today, for instance, I was at Tattersall's investigating a particularly fine hunter. The bidding got too rich for my liking, however." He stopped his tale and looked at Matthew with concern. "You look like something the cat dragged in."

"Thank you."

"No offense meant."

Matthew sighed. "I suppose I should tell you. I'm going to offer for Miss Isabella Larkin soon."

"Congratulations, I believe, are in order," said Spencer sardonically, raising his elegant blond brows. "Although I must say, you do not appear to be anticipating wedded bliss with anything approaching a joyful demeanor."

"It is necessary to be wed, and I am doing so. It is a business proposition. No cause for dissolving into unseemly shows of emotion."

"Oh, I didn't say you were unemotional. Just not joyful. From the look of you, I'd say you were murderous."

Matthew frowned across the table. "I am simply resigned. My uncle will have his wish, Isabella will be able to play mistress of the manor, and I will be left once more to go my way in peace."

"How did Lady Clarissa react to your momentous news?"

Matthew's frown deepened into a full-fledged scowl. "I have not had the opportunity to share the tidings with Lady Clarissa. She was not available yesterday afternoon when I called. Perhaps today I will be more fortunate. It will also be necessary to have an audience with her father as well." He picked up his wine goblet, drained it, and refilled it from the half-full decanter on the table.

Spencer eyed him dubiously. "If you have all of that ahead of you this afternoon, you might be wise to refrain from the wine. You may need all your faculties about you to cope with a weeping miss and her disappointed papa."

"I hardly think Lady Clarissa will be weeping. She has made it quite clear to me lately that she wishes nothing more to do with me. It should be a short call. And as for her papa, he will not dare to play the affronted party with me. He is active in the House of Lords, and has often expressed his hope that my eventual political career will be useful to both of us."

"I see. Then there is no cause to view your afternoon at Denham House with alarm."

"None at all," Matthew confirmed, taking another long draught of wine from his glass. "None at all."

# TWELVE

Perhaps it was just as well that Lady Clarissa had, again, been "out" when he called upon her this afternoon, Matthew reflected that evening, as his carriage bumped along the streets of Mayfair. He really had been in no shape whatsoever for the task at hand. By the time he had left White's, his ill-humor had increased, no doubt due to Spence's lack of sympathy for his situation. His friend, with his falderal about happy marriages, was as flighty-minded as Clarissa, he thought sourly. All well and good for Spencer to have high-flown romantic dreams. Spence was a fourth son with a small but adequate income from his father. He had no need to marry quickly, or even particularly well.

Well, Clarissa would damned well be "in" for him tomorrow, he thought grimly, if he had to keep watch on Denham House all afternoon to catch sight of her. Otherwise, she would just have to read about his engagement in the *Morning Post*, like everyone else. He had no time for foolish feminine games.

His coachman pulled up before the door of the Larkins' home in Hanover Square, and Matthew jumped lightly from his carriage. Swiftly, he was admitted to the elegant hall, and Miss Isabella Larkin emerged within seconds to greet him. He noted with approval her rich blue gown and becoming, if somewhat overblown, hairstyle.

"Good evening, my lord," she said demurely, holding out both her hands. He clasped them in his briefly, then raised one to his lips. She smiled at him, but the warmth of that smile did not quite reach her eyes.

"Mama has voiced a desire to accompany us to Vauxhall this evening, as it is such a beautiful night. Would such an arrangement inconvenience you, my lord?"

Suppressing an overwhelming urge to groan, he tried to bestow his most charming smile on Miss Larkin. "Of course not. She is most welcome."

As if she had been listening at the door, Isabella's mother, Lady Simpson, emerged promptly from the adjacent drawing room. "My dear Lord Langdon," she gushed. "I sincerely hope you do not mind my company on your excursion this evening. It has been years since I have ventured out to Vauxhall, but you must understand that on an evening such as this, I simply could not resist the opportunity. And to travel in such exalted and charming company was the most appealing part of the idea." She bestowed an indulgent smile upon him.

He assumed that the tendency to smile with the lips only, not the eyes, must be a family trait.

Soon, the party was comfortably settled in Langdon's carriage for the drive to Vauxhall. For the duration of the trip, Lady Simpson kept up a steady stream of light conversation, trading *on-dits* with her daughter, commenting upon the clothes and lives of acquaintances in passing carriages, waxing enthusiastic about the weather, and fawning over Lord Langdon's carriage and character. Isabella strove mightily to add her comments to her mother's seamless flow of conversation. The result was somewhat overwhelming.

Matthew thought he would go mad before they arrived.

Before that unhappy circumstance, his coachman slowed the carriage as it merged with the scores of other conveyances approaching the main entrance to the gardens. Matthew alighted from the carriage and assisted the two ladies to the ground, then they joined the festive procession through the main gates.

As they strolled along the wide, shadowy Grand Walk, Matthew listened half-attentively to the prattle of his companions, while keenly observing their fellow pleasure-seekers in London's most popular garden. It was, he decided, simply the Hyde Park carriage crowd on foot. The same bright pleasantries were exchanged, the same sly examinations of frocks and hats and hairstyles were carried out. He greeted any number of acquaintances from Eton and White's. Those squiring young ladies were behaving with more decorum and restraint than he had previously observed them capable of at either the school or the gentlemen's club. There were also young bucks, however, roaming the grounds in rowdy squads. He suspected that they had already sampled the notorious Vauxhall punch.

His companions had also been avidly involved in greeting acquaintances. Really, he thought idly, it mattered not whom one accompanied to Vauxhall, as the entire evening was spent conversing with people in other parties.

Suddenly, an excited cry from Lady Simpson caught his attention. "Why Major Stokes! It has been many a year since I have had the pleasure of greeting you!"

Matthew turned to observe a red-faced, middle-aged man in evening dress approaching. His attention did not center for long on the gentleman, however, for he quickly recognized the two young ladies Major Stokes was proudly escorting. His face flamed briefly as he locked eyes with Clarissa. She, for once, had the good grace to cast her eyes downward.

Matthew barely acknowledged the introductions as his mind reeled with livid thoughts. It certainly had not taken Lady Clarissa long to acquire another admirer, he thought savagely.

And this very afternoon that obsequious Shaftoe had had the gall to inform him that Lady Clarissa was in bed with a megrim! Ill, indeed!

Perhaps it would not be so difficult to inform Lady Clarissa of his impending marriage after all.

"But of course we must sit together for supper," he heard Isabella's mama exclaim effusively.

"It would be my pleasure, my lady," replied Major Stokes.

Matthew cast a quick glance at Clarissa and was gratified to see a look of sheer horror cross her face. No wonder she was terrified to share a table with him, after her shameful behavior lately.

He noted that Lady Anne was observing him thoughtfully. He wondered how much she knew.

The little party made its way to one of the small supper boxes that blustered around the grove. Miss Larkin, her mother, and Major Stokes did not seem to notice the uncomfortable silence that had descended on their companions. It was not surprising, as the major showed every sign of matching Lady Simpson in loquaciousness.

"I am most happy to see you again, my lady," he was saying at the minute. "And Miss Larkin! I cannot contain my astonishment at your transformation. The last time we met, you were but a young miss in the schoolroom."

"Several years can work wonders in a young lady's countenance . . . and knowledge," replied Isabella in a demure voice, but her fluttering eyelashes belied the innocence of her words.

"It is not wise for a lady to become too knowledgeable," he warned her laughingly.

"But certainly it behooves her to gain enough wisdom to render herself fascinating to a gentleman. That is the main role of the gentle sex, is it not?" She snapped open her ivory fan.

As Matthew watched Isabella flirt openly with Major Stokes, he realized he felt not one whit of jealousy. A tinge of disgust, perhaps—she was so flagrantly obvious in her tricks—but he mainly watched her as though she were an actor in a particularly bad play.

"And how are you enjoying the park this evening, my lord?" Lady Anne's voice broke into his musings.

"As well as can be expected."

"One's choice of company is indeed the making of an outing at Vauxhall," she remarked cryptically, with a knowing gleam in her eye. He could not determine whether she referred to Miss Larkin and her mother or to Lady Clarissa.

"It is hardly a matter of choice, it seems, whom one accompanies here, as the most unlikely dinner companions emerge out of the air."

"How peculiar! I was just thinking the same thing myself."

Throughout this exchange, Clarissa had stared blankly out at the grove, resolutely silent. She had not even bothered to remove the red cloak draped around her shoulders. Matthew had no intention of letting her escape her social duties so effortlessly.

"I trust you are feeling better, Lady Clarissa?" he asked with mock solicitousness. She looked at him blankly.

"Your megrim," he prompted. "It does not seem to be troubling you this evening."

She colored. "Yes, my lord. It is greatly improved. I am sorry I was not able to receive you this afternoon." She paused, then continued in a rush. "I do, however, wish to speak to you on a matter of some import."

"Perhaps, after supper, we could take a stroll around the gardens?" The words were innocuous, but the undertone was harsh.

Clarissa stared at him, wide-eyed. "I hardly think that would be appropriate, my lord. You came in the company of Miss Larkin, after all. She might take offense."

"I hardly think that likely," he observed dryly, observing that lady as she continued her open flirtation with Major Stokes. "Besides, I thought you had relinquished your role as my etiquette instructor."

Clarissa looked into her lap, where her hands were torturing a linen table napkin. "You are correct, of course, my lord."

"I believe, Lady Clarissa, that that is the first time you have ever acknowledged that I am right about anything."

"Perhaps. But it will not be the last, I can assure you."

Before he could find out the meaning behind that oblique comment, two things happened simultaneously: a servant arrived with their extravagantly overpriced supper of ham and cold chicken, and Isabella's mama begged his opinion on the unusual waistcoat sported by a passing gentleman.

The meal passed without remarkable incident. As the party enjoyed slices of cheese and glasses of arrack, Major Stokes said to Lady Simpson, "I say, my dear, would you and your charming daughter accompany me on a constitutional? You are welcome to join us too, if you like," he added, almost as an afterthought, to Lady Anne.

She glanced briefly at Clarissa, who nodded almost imperceptibly. "Thank you, Major Stokes, I should be delighted," she replied.

"It would be lovely if you would join us," Isabella's mama said to Matthew with a concerned air. "We do not wish to abandon you."

"Do not concern yourself about me," said Matthew shortly. "Lady Clarissa and I shall sit here and watch the fashionable world go by."

"We shan't be long, my lord," said Lady Simpson, her pale face creased with worry.

"Please, take your time," he said wearily. Isabella, he noted, had not seemed at all concerned about his lack of interest in the excursion.

As the little party moved off into the grove, Matthew barked, "There was something you wished to discuss with me, Lady Clarissa?"

She took a deep breath, and then looked him straight in the eye. "Yes, my lord. I wish to apologize. I behaved most frightfully the other evening."

"Yes, you did," he conceded. "What, exactly, is it that makes you regret your actions now?"

Her gaze did not waver, although her voice was unsteady as she said, "I do not blame you for being furious with me. In answer to your question, it was Mr. Sherrington himself. He proved the truth of your accusations against him. He . . . he asked me for five hundred pounds as he escorted me home from Almack's."

Matthew stared at her in astonishment. Despite his theories about Sherrington, he had not believed the man would be so brazen. The thought of him boldly asking Clarissa for money made Matthew's blood boil.

"And what did you tell him?"

Clarissa gaped at him. "What should I have told him? I informed him, of course, that I do not have access to funds of that sort, and that if I had, I would not lavish them on one such as himself."

"And how did Sherrington react?"

"He was most upset. He accused me of misleading him, when really I had done nothing of the sort. I was most put out by the entire encounter." She paused again. "There would have been no need for it, if I had listened to you. My apologies again, my lord."

"Stop apologizing, Lady Clarissa. The matter is over and done with. I hope, however, that you are not trying to make amends in the hopes of reviving our former . . . association?"

"Do you wish to do so, my lord?" she asked blandly, her eyes hooded.

"No. I am most indebted to you for your advice, and you will be pleased to know it has made a suitable suitor of me. I plan to offer for Miss Larkin within the next few days."

A strange, indefinable shadow passed across Clarissa's face, but before he could ponder its meaning, it had disappeared.

"Congratulations, my lord," she murmured. "I wish you and your intended every wedded happiness."

"As long as we share a civil and fruitful union, I shall be satisfied," he said, the words sounding pompous to his own ears. Gad, this interview was becoming most uncomfortable.

"I hope, for your sake, that your marriage is much more than that. I know you place no value on such things, my lord, but it seems unfortunate that you should be denied your share of joy." As she looked at him across the table in the dim light, he could have sworn her eyes were bright with unshed tears.

Nonsense, he told himself. "Please, Lady Clarissa, do not burden me with your romantic notions. I shall inform your father of my intentions tomorrow." He paused, clearing his throat. "I wish you luck in your

own pursuit of, er, joy. Ah, here come our companions," he said with relief as the party reappeared. Lady
Anne walked some steps behind the other three, who
were engaged in a raucous conversation punctuated
by Miss Larkin's giggle and her mama's shrill laugh.

Matthew sighed audibly.

"Your demeanor does not seem to be that of a man
eagerly awaiting his intended's approach," Clarissa remarked acidly.

"That is no concern of yours," he muttered as he
rose to greet Miss Larkin.

# THIRTEEN

The music was pleasant enough, Matthew supposed, but the small gilt chair upon which he sat was becoming increasingly uncomfortable, and the atmosphere in the room was close and hot. Someone nearby was wearing a great quantity of scent, and the constant whiffs of it were making Matthew's head buzz.

At the front of Lady Simpson's drawing room, a perspiring pianist continued doggedly through one of Herr Beethoven's latest piano concertos. But for the attention the festively attired crowd was paying to the performance, he might have been playing children's tunes, Matthew mused.

Seated beside him, Isabella had been engaged in whispered conversation for the last five minutes with an older woman wearing a bright green velvet dress and a shimmering diamond necklace, who waved a large plumed fan incessantly. From the bits of conversation he caught, he believed they were talking about a party that had taken place last summer in Berkshire.

Behind him, two young bucks had been swinging their feet idly against the back of his chair and noisily taking pinches of snuff. And in front of him, an elderly gentleman had fallen asleep on his bored wife's shoulder. Occasionally, he snuffled quietly and shifted position.

All in all, Matthew was heartily relieved when the pianist finished the piece to a smattering of polite applause. Stiffly, he rose from his chair, stretching his long legs.

"Please excuse me, my lord," Isabella said quickly as she, too, rose. "I must speak with my mother a moment. Perhaps there is some way we can cool this room before the next performance."

"A most worthy objective," he replied dryly.

"A table of refreshments has been set up in the next room," she added. "If you wish to sample some of them, I shall join you there presently."

"Of course, Miss Larkin," he said indifferently, as she glided off in search of Lady Simpson.

Left to his own devices, he followed several other guests into the adjoining drawing room. Lord Simpson's townhouse in Hanover Square was inviting and functional, he noted, but it was much smaller than Stonecourt and had little of the Langdon family home's opulence. Somehow, he suspected Isabella was already making plans for the grand entertainments she could hold in his home. It was of little import to him. He would be spending most of his time at the House, at White's, or in the country, he reminded himself.

Idly, he eyed the glittering crowd gathered around the refreshment table. There were many people he recognized, but few he cared to converse with. Then suddenly, he spied Piers Sherrington deep in conversation with the Dowager Duchess of Aylesbury, a white-haired, stout woman whose high-pitched giggle frequently echoed over the room. His eyes narrowed.

He didn't realize he had been staring until the poet left his elderly companion and moved across the room towards him. "Good evening, my lord," he said in a neutral voice. "You seemed most intrigued by my conversation with the dowager duchess. I thought I would come over to investigate the cause of your concern. Is my cravat, perhaps, askew? Or was my companion laughing a bit too loudly? I suppose I really must correct that habit of hers, someday," he remarked, as if to himself.

Matthew eyed the younger man with distaste. "Are you planning on an extended friendship with the dowager duchess?"

"Oh, yes," Mr. Sherrington remarked candidly. "She's frightfully wealthy, you know, and quite mad as well. However, she considers me amusing company. I think she sees me as something of a favorite pet. We have been spending quite a bit of time together in the last few weeks. I do believe our association could turn into a mutually profitable, long-term relationship."

"You are not considering offering for her?" Matthew asked, with undisguised astonishment. Most of the *haute ton* was protective of the dowager duchess, recognizing in her instability an echo of the madness that had finally overtaken their own king. Matthew was astonished that her son, the Duke of Aylesbury, would even consider approving such a preposterous union.

"You needn't look so offended," Piers replied in a pettish tone. "Whyever shouldn't I? We suit each other's needs most admirably. She has bags of blunt with which to support me, in return for which I am simply required to regale her with witty tales. Her family, I am sure, will be more than willing to have me take some of the responsibility for her care. And her . . . ahem . . . demands upon me will be slight. We both understand that I shall be free to maintain other liaisons elsewhere."

Matthew felt sick as he looked at the young poet. His earlier distaste was rapidly growing into outright revulsion. "Do you have no other concern than money in the arrangement of your marital affairs?"

"The Dowager Duchess of Aylesbury and I understand each other perfectly," Piers replied airily. "I am looking for money, and she is looking for status and an amusing companion. Are not all society marriages arranged along such pragmatic lines? They are generally marriages of advantage, rather than love matches." He paused thoughtfully. "Although, perhaps, you are a romantic man. I seem to recall that you spent some time in the last few months pursuing the attentions of the fair Lady Clarissa Denham, and she can offer you neither wealth nor status. Although her father does outrank you, the family has fallen upon difficult times."

"I seem to have been privy to that information sooner than you were yourself," Matthew replied through gritted teeth. How much social disgrace would befall him, he wondered, if he slapped this disgusting parasite right here in Lady Simpson's drawing room?

"And I see you have taken similar action," the poet

replied guilelessly. He nodded toward the doorway, where Isabella Larkin had appeared. She was scanning the room, presumably looking for Matthew. "Miss Larkin, to be certain, has a much more prodigious dowry to offer. I am only sorry I did not think to pursue her first myself. Although I daresay it is her beauty, more than her blunt, that has drawn your attention."

"Get out of my sight, you wretched idiot, before I box your ears." Matthew was quickly losing his tenuous grasp on his temper.

"Don't see why you're so affronted," Piers said sulkily. "Anyone can see it's not the girl's brains or charm you're marrying her for. I must say, you are terribly naive, for all your worldly airs." With that, Piers turned on his heel and returned to the chortling dowager duchess.

Matthew stalked out of the room through a pair of French doors that had been opened to let in some of the fresh night air. He sat on a bench in the tiny garden and pondered Sherrington's ugly words.

Was his courtship of Isabella as venal and crude as Sherrington's shameless pursuit of the Dowager Duchess of Aylesbury? He thought not. Isabella and he understood the purpose of it. They knew it was a business arrangement. But had not Sherrington said the same thing of his possible marriage to the dowager duchess? Why, then, did Matthew find that liaison so repugnant?

Perhaps it was due to the age difference between the partners, or the fact that the elderly dowager duchess was not in complete possession of her faculties.

No, he slowly admitted to himself, he was little better

than the greedy poet. His motives simply had the gloss of societal approval on them.

But what else was there for it? he asked himself bleakly.

There's always Clarissa, a tiny voice sounded in his head. With time, perhaps she could become reconciled to another proposal.

He shook his head in frustration. Where had that thought come from? The last thing he needed was the volatile Clarissa and her headful of romantic notions.

The last thing he needed, he acknowledged, was a woman he might grow to love. Such a woman had brought his uncle nothing but grief. How could he have forgotten that?

He had been putting off his visit to Lord Wickford, ostensibly to give Lady Clarissa more time to find a suitor. But, he admitted to himself, some tiny part of him had been unwilling to give up the possibility of offering for her again at a future date.

He had to start putting his life in order, he admonished himself. He had told Clarissa she must be realistic. Now, like Sherrington, he must do the same.

"There you are, my lord." He heard Isabella's clear voice behind him. "I wondered where you had disappeared to."

"I needed a breath of fresh air."

She sat down beside him on the narrow stone bench. Her hair shone in the moonlight, and her blue eyes were wide and clear. Despite her beauty and the fragrance of young roses and lavender floating from the shadowy reaches of the garden, he felt no romantic urge to steal a kiss from her young lips—as he had from Clarissa's on that unusual evening at Stonecourt.

What he felt, instead, was a profound weariness.

He realized Isabella had been speaking to him, and asked her to repeat herself.

"I merely said, my lord, that we should return to the house. The next performance is about to begin."

All of life was beginning to feel like a performance to him, Matthew reflected sourly as they returned to the stuffy music room. He would be heartily glad to be done with this tiresome courtship ritual. Tomorrow, he would take the first step. He would seek an audience with Clarissa's father.

Clarissa sat listlessly on a long, low sofa in her mother's mahogany-paneled drawing room. Usually, she thoroughly enjoyed her mother's soirées. But this evening, the spirited conversation seemed to wash over her like an uncaring tide. She responded when required, but sat in uncharacteristic silence for most of the evening.

Her thoughts, as they had so often these days, turned to the Earl of Langdon. Why had he not spoken to her father? she wondered helplessly. Lord Wickford was growing increasingly curious about the fact that Matthew had not visited recently. Clarissa had found herself creating elaborate excuses for the earl's prolonged absences, as well as Mr. Sherrington's. Since their unpleasant interlude in the carriage on the way home from Almack's, Clarissa had not set eyes on the poet.

Her father, she feared, was becoming suspicious.

Shaking her head, she tried dutifully to involve herself in the conversation, a spirited debate about the identity of the author of such popular anonymous novels as *Guy Mannering* and the new *Waverly*.

"Who could it be, who is so fearful of fame as to hide his name from the public?" asked the quick-witted Duchess of Landsborough.

"Perhaps a vicar, or a politician, who believes a reputation as a novelist would sully his sterling image," replied Mr. Brownleigh, a pleasant young man sitting opposite Clarissa.

"I can't imagine anyone who would disavow such wonderful, romantic stories," the duchess replied.

"Perhaps the author, whoever he or she might be, has simply come to the conclusion that novels are so far removed from ordinary life that it is a reprehensible profession to write them. After all, such writings might just convince some poor, unworldly souls that romance really does exist in the world," Clarissa said suddenly, with such bitterness that the duchess stared at her in consternation.

Clarissa, realizing her *faux pas*, added quickly, "Please, forgive me. I have read several novels of late that have not been worth the coins it cost to borrow them from the circulating library." She tried to smile convincingly. "I fear it has given me an uncharacteristically harsh view of novels in general. But I am sure, if *Guy Mannering* is as enthralling as you say, it shall restore my former esteem of the art form." Although her words seemed to appease the gathering, she doubted the truth of them even as she spoke them.

Piers Sherrington's perfidy, and Lord Langdon's practicality, had forced her to see the world more clearly. Never again would she have anyone tell her she was romantic and naive.

The evening, to Clarissa's mind, dragged on interminably, but it finally drew to a close. As the last of the guests left, Lady Wickford looked at her daughter with concern. "Are you feeling well, my dear?" she inquired. "You were not in your usual fine form tonight."

"I'm sorry, Mama. I am somewhat distracted these days."

"Is it anything you would like to discuss with me?" Sophia Denham's eyes were kind and worried.

Clarissa hesitated. She had been unwilling to tell anyone of her distasteful encounter with Mr. Sherrington and her shocking display of bad manners with Lord Langdon. However, the more she kept the unpalatable events to herself, the more they preyed on her soul. And the more she worried that they would soon come to her father's attention.

Suddenly anxious to share her burden, she told the whole ignominious tale to her mother. Lady Wickford's eyes widened in shock as Clarissa described Piers' demand for money, and filled with tears as Clarissa told of her final ignominious encounter with Lord Langdon at Vauxhall.

"Oh, my poor child!" she exclaimed. "If only there was something I could do."

"Thank you, Mama, but there is nothing anyone can do," Clarissa said morosely. "I brought this entire debacle on my own head. It is time to become realistic, and find a suitor quickly. Do you suppose Mr. Brown-leigh might be interested in me?" she asked hopefully. "He seems to be a nice young man."

Sophia Denham sighed. "He is, my dear, but I urge you not to simply pursue any available gentleman simply to appease your father. Even if you have to go to Yorkshire and wait hand and foot on your crotchety great-aunt, it cannot be a worse fate than marriage to a man you do not love." She paused, then added for emphasis, "Believe me. I know."

Clarissa closed her eyes wearily. "I really do not know what is the worst fate anymore. I just wish people would let me be. I am perfectly happy the way I am."

# FOURTEEN

"Good afternoon," said the Marquess of Wickford oppressively as Clarissa entered his study and closed the door.

"Good afternoon, Father." Clarissa stood next to a battered wing chair.

"Sit down, Clarissa." It was a command, not a request.

With a sense of foreboding, Clarissa sank into the soft, worn leather. Her father said nothing, just continued to stare at her. Finally, she could stand it no longer. "Why did you call me here, Father?" she said in a strained voice.

"To discover the reasons Lord Langdon has cried off," he spat, slamming his fist down on the mahogany desk with such force that she jumped. "What on earth could you possibly have done? He came to call on me not twenty minutes ago, and said simply that you and he did not suit. What am I to infer from that?"

"It is just as he said, Father. We did not feel it would be an advantageous match."

Clarissa thought rapidly. At least, to her father's knowledge, Mr. Sherrington was still considering offering for her hand. Perhaps she could forestall her father's anger for a few more days.

"You seem to have developed some skill in alienating your suitors." Lord Wickford's voice sliced into her thoughts. Carelessly, he tossed a copy of the *Morning Post* across the desk to her. It was folded back to the social announcements page. Dreading what she would find there, she looked down and read of the engagement of Mr. Piers Sherrington to the Dowager Duchess of Aylesbury. She was more than twice his age, quite mad and formidably rich.

Her world was collapsing around her, but strangely all Clarissa could feel was mute sympathy for the dowager duchess.

"It is most unfortunate for you that things did not work out," her father ground out. "I will give you a few days to get your affairs in order and to say your farewells to your friends here in Town. By the end of the week, I expect you to be ready to depart for Great-Aunt Agatha's."

"But, Father . . ."

"I will brook no disagreement." The marquess' eyes glittered like obsidian as he stared at his daughter. "When I arranged the match with Lord Langdon, I told you the terms. You must know that, above all things, I am a man of my word."

Clarissa, thinking quickly, seized the first germ of a plan that came into her head. "May I visit with Emily for a few days on my way to Great-Aunt Agatha's? Once I am settled in the north, it will be much more difficult to visit Hampshire."

Her father's aspect softened slightly. "I suppose it

would be no great matter for you to visit your sister for a few weeks. The delay will give your great-aunt time to prepare to receive you."

"Thank you, Father," she said sadly. "May I please be excused?"

"Yes, go ahead. I will write to Great-Aunt Agatha at once."

Clarissa strode briskly out of the library. She, also, had several letters to write.

In her room, she sat down at her small cherrywood desk, and gazed out on the bustling street below. An elegant barouche clattered by, and the laughter of two young women out walking with their maids floated up to her. How she would miss London! Suddenly everything about it seemed more dear to her: Colburn's circulating library, afternoon visits with Anne, Astley's circus, Drury Lane, even the shops of Oxford Street. It was difficult to believe she would never see any of it again.

Of course, if she went to live with Great-Aunt Agatha, there was the chance that she could return to London occasionally, perhaps to stay with Anne or other friends.

But she wasn't going to Yorkshire. Carefully, she withdrew two sheets of paper from her writing desk. She wrote one letter to her former schoolmistress Miss Hilson, asking if any positions in Canada were still available. In her second letter, she asked her sister Emily if she could stay with her in Hampshire for a few weeks while awaiting a ship to take her abroad.

Bleakly, she sealed both letters and returned downstairs to place both of them on the table in the foyer.

* * *

Later that afternoon, Clarissa found herself in a decidedly unsavory part of the city.

"I really don't think we should be here, Lady Clarissa," her maid Betty murmured uneasily. "What would his lordship say if he knew we was here?"

"He will never know, so there is no need to worry," Clarissa said stoutly. Nevertheless, she pulled her bright red wool cloak more closely about her and increased her pace until Betty cried out in protest.

Betty had not been the only one to be unnerved. The coachman who had driven them here had protested vehemently all the way across London, and had increased his supplications as the carriage crossed the bridge across the Thames.

"Ye can't do this, Lady Clarissa!" he had cried. "I won't be able to accompany ye once we get deep into the neighborhood. This rig won't go down them narrow streets, and if I leave it alone it'll surely be stolen. And then where will we be?"

Reluctantly, Clarissa had fallen back upon her superior status to convince the man to do her bidding.

"Remember, Watkins, that I can have you fired if I so choose," she had said firmly, hating herself for the words. She loathed those who used their power to threaten their servants into submission. But today, she was desperate. She had to make this trip.

Clarissa had never in her life visited this section of London, but she knew from listening to her brother's school friends that Spitalfields was the place to go if you wanted to pawn something cheaply and anonymously. Several of them had run up enormous gambling debts and thus had an intimate knowledge of these grimy streets. After receiving more than one leering glance from men lounging against the crumbling walls of decrepit row houses, however, Clarissa had no wish to become closely acquainted with the neighborhood. She vowed to enter the first pawnshop she saw, no matter how disreputable it appeared.

Luckily, she quickly found such an establishment, which was as dingy and unappealing as she had feared. The small, dusty display window was crowded with cheap tarnished trinkets. With a confidence she did not feel, she boldly opened the shop's dirt-streaked door. Betty, looking fearfully about, followed her closely.

As she entered, a stringy-looking man unfolded himself from behind the counter. He openly inspected her from bonnet to boots before inquiring with unmasked curiosity, "How may I help you, miss?"

Swallowing her distaste, she marched up to the counter and opened her reticule. "I have some goods I would like to pawn sir."

He gaped at her, then a knowing look came over his face. "You are in need of some immediate . . . pin money?"

"Yes."

"Of course, I will give you a fair rate for your items." He paused. "When you have the cash, would you be looking for the services of . . . a discreet professional?"

"What do you mean?" Clarissa's voice was puzzled.

"Well, my cousin, for instance, is a respected midwife. She has wide knowledge of everything to do with childbirth and . . . related matters."

As his meaning dawned on her, Clarissa gasped. "How dare you make such an insinuation? It is perfectly monstrous! Do you abuse all your customers in this fashion?" Angrily, she snapped shut her reticule and prepared to leave.

Mr. Jones, sensing he had made a grievous error, hastened to reassure his prosperous-looking patron. "Please forgive me, miss. I assure you I didn't mean any harm. I just thought that if you were looking for help, I could give my cousin a little extra custom." As Clarissa continued to move toward the door, he pointed out quickly, "The next pawnshop is a full half-block down the road. Surely you must have noticed that this is an unsuitable area for a young woman to walk in alone. You'd be best advised to deal with me, ma'am."

She stopped at the door as Betty piped up, "I agree, my lady."

Reluctantly, she turned back to the odious shopkeeper, opened her reticule again, and withdrew a small bundle wrapped in a handkerchief. When she unwrapped the fine lawn, the man behind the counter picked among the few bits of jewelry therein with a practiced hand.

"These should net you a fair price," he said casually.

With a sigh, Clarissa removed the emerald ring from her finger and added it to the small collection. The proprietor's beady eyes glittered. "Now that," he said with barely concealed excitement, "is definitely worth something."

"I should hope so," Clarissa said bitterly. "It is a family heirloom."

"My loans are for one half the worth of the item, so I'll give you one hundred pounds for it."

"It is worth at least three hundred and fifty," Clarissa shot back. "The emerald, as you can see, is a particularly fine cut." She hoped he could not see her hands shaking. She was well-used to bargaining with shopkeepers, but usually as a buyer, not a seller. And not with so much at stake.

"I doubt that it is worth such a price," he snorted.

"Fine. Despite the risk, I believe I will take my custom elsewhere." But before she could sweep her jewelry back into her reticule, the shopkeeper relented.

"I'll give you one hundred and thirty, and not tuppence more."

"I believe we have a bargain," Clarissa said, struggling to keep the relief out of her voice. Her original estimate had been highly exaggerated, she knew. The sum he had offered was quite adequate.

Her other pieces brought moderate prices, and when the transaction was finished Clarissa placed one hundred and eighty pounds into her almost-empty reticule. She left the shop as hastily as she could and walked briskly along the narrow street. This time, Betty made no complaint as she struggled to keep up with her mistress. They emerged onto the main thoroughfare with no mishaps. The coachman, looking vastly relieved to see Clarissa and her maid, quickly collected them.

On the way back to Denham House, Clarissa swore

both servants to absolute silence about her after-noon errand.

"I see that Sherrington has found richer fish to fry," Spencer Willoughby remarked as he eyed the billiard table along the length of his cue.

"So I read in the *Post,*" Matthew replied with stud-ied indifference. Inwardly, though, he was cursing himself for his bad timing. Clarissa's father had seemed on the verge of an apoplexy during their in-terview last week, and Matthew had been at a loss to understand it until he saw the engagement notice in the *Post* that same morning. He surmised that Wick-ford had considered Sherrington a second choice for Clarissa, and had been damnably incensed to see both her prospects evaporate at once. Clarissa herself had likely borne the brunt of his wrath. To his annoyance, he felt a wave of sympathy for her. Resolutely, he stamped it out. She had brought all these woes on herself with her stubbornness. She would have to live with the consequences. It was unlikely her father would inflict any lasting reprisal on her.

Spencer missed the shot and cheerfully moved aside so that Matthew could line up his own. It was blissfully quiet and calm in Spencer's father's billiard room, Matthew reflected. He had had quite enough of emo-tional scenes over the last few days, between Clarissa and her father. Yes, he was well-rid of the pair of them.

"I was half-expecting to see your own notice in the paper. I thought you were on the verge of offering for Miss Larkin several weeks ago," Spencer remarked innocently, then grinned as Matthew completely missed his shot.

"Yes, I was," Matthew said with a gusty sigh. "I am just waiting for a propitious moment."

"Oh, but how can you bear to forestall Lady Simpson's joy for even one day? You know, surely, that she will be most appreciative when she learns her daughter is to become a countess."

"Believe me, Spencer, I am well aware of that fact. I just hope I can survive her outpouring of gratitude," he said dryly. "She is not noted for her quiet manner."

Spencer, across the table, hooted with laughter. "As always, you are a master of understatement." Deftly, he lined up his shot and pocketed two balls. "Sorry, my friend, but I have defeated you yet again. Your game is off today."

"I am a bit tired this afternoon," Matthew said. "As a matter of fact, I believe I will return home. I have some materials I must read for an upcoming debate in the House. Thank you for your hospitality."

"Well, never let it be said I stood in the way of affairs of state," Spencer said with a laugh. "And please let me know when the date of the wedding is to be. I could not bear to be the last to hear the joyful news."

Matthew grimaced as he replaced his cue on the rack and put on his jacket, but did not reply. Suddenly, he felt tired beyond words.

Collecting his horse from the stable, he rode briskly through Mayfair, eager to get home. Several streets from Stonecourt, however, he was caught in a crush of people who had stopped to observe some sort of altercation on the pavement.

"I have the evidence right here in my hand, you filthy urchin," a shrill woman's voice rose above the crowd. "What do you have to say for yourself?"

"I'm sorry ma'am, truly I is, but me mam's so sick and the beadle wants to put her in the poorhouse and she'll die in there, my lady, and I really needs the money." The torrent of words poured out in a thin, reedy voice. Matthew paused. Had he not heard that voice somewhere before? But where?

Edging closer to the melee, he looked down to see the young boy who had taken care of his horse when he visited the Spitalfields pawn shop. The child, red with shame and trembling dreadfully, was down on his knees before a stout, imperious woman swathed in crimson velvet whom Matthew recognized as Lady Hammond. A reticule obviously just retrieved from the boy dangled from her hand.

"I am sure all you young cutpurses have some sort of pitiful story prepared to tell in the event that you are caught," Lady Hammond's voice boomed. "I am not impressed. I shall call for a Bow Street Runner!"

Impulsively, Matthew called out, "Please reconsider, Lady Hammond."

Immediately, the crowd swiveled to look up at him, and Matthew felt somewhat foolish. Now that he had started, he felt compelled to finish.

"Why, Lord Langdon," Lady Hammond simpered. "How pleasant to see you. But you must not concern yourself with this minor little crime. I can assure you, the situation is well in hand."

"I realize, my lady, that the young lad has committed

a grave offense. But have your belongings been restored to you?"

"Why, yes, due to the quick actions of several gentlemen who caught this petty thief before he could escape." She let a huff of righteous indignation escape her pursed lips.

"As no lasting harm has been done, perhaps it would be most prudent to let the young lad go. No sense bothering Bow Street. They have their hands full dealing with more serious crimes. I will take it upon myself to escort the child back to his home and impress upon him that it would be unwise to attempt such an act again."

"But, Lord Langdon . . ." Lady Hammond began, confused. Her desire for vindication was clearly warring with her natural inclination to pander to a man of higher station. Social training eventually won the day. "Perhaps you are right, my lord, although I must say your offer is most unusual."

"Consider it my good turn for the day," he said dryly. To one of the bystanders, he added, "Please hand the boy up to me." Gently, Matthew lifted the sobbing child onto his saddle.

Once they were away from the chattering crowd, the boy lifted his tear-stained face up to look at his protector. "Why, guv'nor!" he said. "I di'n't recognize youse." Then, after an embarrassed pause, he added, "Thank you, sir. They'd have had me head on a pike, so they would. An' I was telling the truth. Me mam's dreadful ill."

"I knew you weren't lying," Matthew replied. Then, as an afterthought he added, "What's your name?"

"Jackie Marshall." He paused, then confided in a rush, "I came here cuz I knew it was where all the toffs was. It'd take me a month of Sundays to beg enough money 'round home. Me mam needs medicine, that's wot Miz Chumley says. She's our neighbor. So I needed to get some money quick."

"Is your mother at home?" Matthew asked.

Jackie looked up at him incredulously. "Where else would she be, guv'nor? She can't hardly get out of bed."

"If you tell me how to get there, I'll take you back. Perhaps I can help."

The boy's eyes widened. "Don't tell her where you found me. She'd be spittin' mad if she know'd I was stealin'."

"I will be utterly discreet," Matthew assured him.

Jackie's eyebrows came together in a frown. "Does that mean youse won't tell?"

Matthew let out a bark of laughter. "Yes."

Eventually, they reached the neighborhood where Langdon had first met the young lad. Following Jackie's directions, he soon drew up before a dilapidated, one-story house on a narrow street. A window box, obviously installed to give the cheerless dwelling some measure of beauty, held an array of drooping plants.

"Hey, Mick! Come watch the guv'nor's horse, can ye?" Jackie called to one of the urchins who had gathered on the pavement at the approach of the fine horse and its elegant rider.

" 'Course, Jackie." A dusty youngster approached as Matthew swung down from the horse and turned to lift down his young charge. "Hangin' around with the toffs, is youse?"

"He sez he might be able to help me mam," said Jackie candidly. "Keep a good eye on the horse, will youse? Don't get up to any tricks."

"Got me word, Jackie," the other youngster replied seriously. Matthew noted with some amusement the authority his scrappy young friend appeared to wield in the neighborhood.

The unlikely pair entered the house. The living space appeared to consist entirely of one room, which served as kitchen, parlor and sleeping area. As Matthew's eyes adjusted to the gloom, lit only by one sputtering tallow candle, he was able to discern the shape of a thin, middle-aged woman sitting beside a bedframe in the corner. In the bed lay a younger woman, pale and drenched in sweat.

"Aye, Jackie, who be ye bringin' in? Yer mam's in no shape fer visitors." The older woman stood and squinted at the new arrival.

"Shush, Miz Chumley, this here's a friend of mine, Lord Langdon, and he sez he might be able to help me mam."

The neighbor drew closer and peered into the gloom. "Oh, my apologies, my lord," she said with a slight, jerky movement that might have been a curtsy. "I di'n't realize . . ."

"It's quite all right," he said, not unkindly. "What exactly is the nature of the lady's illness?"

"Ah, she's got a turrible fever, my lord, I don't rightly know what it is. I knows my cousin's daughter had sump'thin similar once, and she got something from the apoth'cary and was right as rain."

Matthew peered at the woman asleep in the narrow bed, but his knowledge of matters medical was slight. "I'll send word to my personal physician. He will come as soon as he can and see what can be done." Reaching into his purse he withdrew several heavy coins and pressed them into Mrs. Chumley's hand. "Meanwhile, take this bit of money and buy the boy and his mother something nourishing to eat."

The woman opened her hand and gasped when she saw the gift. "My lord, I couldn't be walking into the shop with money like this. Old Wickens would think I'd been pickin' purses!"

"Don't worry about what people will think. Just be sure you do it."

"But why, my lord? Why is youse . . . why are you bein' so good to strangers?"

Matthew sighed. "Maybe because I felt the need to do something right, for a change. It's been a rarity, lately."

She looked at him with confusion.

"And, Jackie," he said, turning to the young boy who still stood by the door, his eyes fixed unbelievingly on the money in his neighbor's hand, "if you need more money, come to me. Don't go looking for it elsewhere," he said meaningfully, staring the child straight in the eye.

The boy nodded gratefully, acknowledging the fact that Matthew had kept his secret. "Where will I find you, guv'nor?"

Matthew gave him the address, then bid the boy and

Mrs. Chumley a quick goodbye. He had no wish to revel in the role of Lord Bountiful.

Outside, he collected his horse from Jackie's obviously awestruck friend, tossing the lad a shilling. Anxious to leave this neighborhood where every face seemed to stare at him with fascination, he leapt onto the horse and exited the dingy alley quickly.

Shortly before he reached the main thoroughfare, he came upon the pawnshop where he had first found some of Sherrington's goods for sale. Idly, he dismounted and peered in the window, curious to see whether any of the poet's trinkets had been given pride of place in the grimy display window.

Before he noticed anything belonging to Piers, however, his eyes alighted on a glinting emerald ring. A very familiar looking emerald ring.

Suddenly he remembered the ring Clarissa always wore. He stared at the piece again through the window, but could not say with complete certainty that it was the same ring. Clarissa had mentioned that hers was a treasured family heirloom, and that she would only part with it under the most dire circumstances.

Quickly tying his horse Lightning to a nearby post, heedless of the very good chance that the prime thoroughbred might be stolen, he strode into the shop and shouted for the proprietor.

"There's no need to bellow," came a whining voice from the door at the back of the shop. "I'm not deaf." The skinny owner emerged. "Oh, it's you, my lord. Any other trifles you're willing to part with today? That tie pin sold very quickly."

"Who pawned that emerald ring in the window?" Matthew demanded without preamble.

"My lord, you do seem quite curious about my customers these days."

"Don't waste my time. I'll get the information from you one way or another in the end, so let us just be quick about it. Was it a young, dark-haired woman?"

"Could have been," replied the proprietor, leaning his bony forearms on top of a smudged glass display case.

Grinding his teeth with suppressed fury, Matthew spat out, "I want to buy the damned thing, and I'll pay a good price, but only if the seller was the young woman I believe it was. Did she have a pale complexion?"

"Hard to tell. She'd been out in the wind, as I remember. Could have been flushed." Seemingly unconcerned, but with his eyes glittering, Mr. Jones leaned over and began rooting through some boxes below the counter.

In two strides Matthew was across the shop and had grabbed the skinny proprietor by the collar. Yanking him upright, he said fiercely, "Does this, perhaps, jog your memory?" He withdrew his gold pocket watch and waved it before the other man's eyes.

"Yes, my lord," the pawnbroker burst out. "She was in here not more than a month ago. Came with some frightened looking little maid. She was dark, with pale skin, and wore a big red cloak." Matthew nodded briefly. Probably the same garment she had worn the night at Vauxhall.

Jones paused, remembering. "I think the maid's name was Betty, if that's of any use to you."

That clinched it. He had remembered Clarissa mentioning her maid by name on several occasions. "That is useful indeed," he replied tightly, tossing the watch carelessly on the cabinet. "May I have the ring, please?"

Jones picked up the Swiss-made timepiece and caressed it between his stubby fingers as he sauntered to the display window and removed the emerald ring. "There you are, my lord," he said, giving the piece to Matthew. "Pleasure doing business with you."

"Not really, but thank you for your rather grudging assistance," said Matthew ungraciously as he put the ring into his inside breast pocket and strode from the shop.

As he emerged, he noticed several older boys eyeing Lightning speculatively. His fierce glare quickly disabused them of any criminal notions they might have been entertaining, and they slunk away quickly without a backward glance.

Jumping up easily onto Lightning, he took off from the grubby lane at a blind gallop. He could almost feel the ring burning a hole in his pocket. What on earth could be the dire consequences that had forced Clarissa to sell it?

Without thought of what he would do when he got there, Matthew urged his horse through the streets in the direction of Denham House.

# FIFTEEN

"I'm sorry, Lord Langdon, but Lady Clarissa has left town," said the unreadable Shaftoe.

"Left town?" Matthew was nonplussed.

"Yes." The butler's face was stony.

Desperate for some answers, Matthew seized the first possibility that occurred to him. "Is Lady Lucinda at home?"

Shaftoe's eyebrows rose infinitesimally. "Yes, she is in the blue salon. Allow me to summon the house-keeper."

Drumming his fingers on a small Sheraton table, Matthew waited with barely restrained impatience in the foyer for Mrs. Harrison to appear. She, too, eyed him uneasily as she accompanied him and Shaftoe to the blue salon. Well, perhaps it was a bit unusual for a man to call alone on a young chit not even out of the schoolroom. To hell with it, he thought. Let 'em wonder.

"Good afternoon, Lord Langdon," said Lucy with evident surprise as she rose from a small settle, where she had been working on some embroidery. "If you are seeking my sister, I am afraid you will be disappointed. She has left town."

"So I was informed," he said with a brittle smile and a pointed look at the two servants. Shaftoe turned abruptly and disappeared through the open doorway, still radiating disapproval. Mrs. Harrison moved to the farthest corner of the room, looking out the window as Shaftoe himself had done on the day he was forced to play chaperon to Matthew and Clarissa.

Matthew sat down on one of the Queen Anne chairs and looked at Lucy steadily. "Where has she gone?"

"If you must know, she's gone to visit our sister Emily in Hampshire. Then she will continue on to Yorkshire."

"Yorkshire? Whatever for?"

"She's been sent there to live with our great-aunt."

"Sent?" Matthew was more puzzled than ever. "By whom?"

"By Father," said Lucy impatiently. "Did she not tell you? When you arrived originally to offer for her, Father said she had to accept or he would pack her off to Great-Aunt Aggie's. Not that it was much of a choice," added Lucy bluntly. "Aunty is a notorious harridan, although I know that's a terrible thing to say. But she is. She's the only one of us who has any money, however, which is why Rissa's been sent there to live."

"To live?" Matthew echoed in astonishment.

"Father said he couldn't afford to keep her, so it was either marry or leave," said Lucy in a matter-of-fact tone.

"I had no idea . . ." he began faintly.

"Well, it isn't exactly the normal course of family affairs, is it? But Father was adamant. Rissa was beside herself. She's never been much of a one to cry—not like me—but if you had seen her when she left! She hugged me several times, the tears streaming down her face. She kept saying, 'You take care, Lucy.' As though she would never see me again." Lucy frowned. "Yorkshire is far away, but it's not as though she were going to the colonies or some such thing."

The colonies . . . a snippet of an old conversation came back to Matthew's mind. He sat forward intently. "Do you know, by any chance, if Lady Clarissa has written lately to her former schoolmistress?"

It was Lucy's turn to be startled. "Why yes, she has. However did you know? I happened to notice such a letter sitting in the foyer, about a week before Clarissa left for Emily's. Why do you ask?" Her young face was troubled, as if she suspected something sinister.

Matthew had no intention of alarming her, however, until he was certain of the truth of the awful picture he had begun to see in his mind's eye. "Just a hunch," he said smoothly. "I've often heard that young women become very close to their schoolmistresses, and I thought perhaps Clarissa might have written to hers to inform her of her change of address." It was not a very convincing lie, and he could tell by Lucy's face that she had not believed a word of it.

"Perhaps," she said in a neutral voice. "But if you think there is any other reason, my lord, you would let me know, would you not?"

"If there is any other reason, you'll know soon enough," said Matthew vaguely. "And now, would you be kind enough to tell me where in Hampshire, exactly, your sister Emily lives?"

* * *

Clarissa put down the morning paper with a sigh. She and Emily were lingering over coffee in the small, sunny breakfast room at Tuncliffe Manor.

"What's wrong, Clare?" her older sister asked with concern.

"Nothing at all," she replied brightly with a slight, forced smile. "Why do you ask?"

"Perhaps because you have yet again perused the paper, found no news of Lord Langdon's supposed betrothal, and still appear distressed. Are you more upset because he has not yet spoken for the lovely Miss Larkin, or because you fear he still will?"

Clarissa colored at her sister's apt assessment of affairs. "It is rather unnerving staying with you, Emily. It is almost as though you have a window into my mind. Yes, it is true that there is no news of Lord Langdon in the announcements. I was sighing because I find my continued interest in that gentleman somewhat tiresome. And yet I cannot seem to help myself." She smiled more broadly.

It had been delightful to spend such an extended period of time with her elder sister, Clarissa reflected, even if the atmosphere in the isolated manor was not always completely welcoming. When Simon was absent, as was more often than not the case, she and Emily enjoyed themselves thoroughly. Clarissa gave her sister all the news she knew of the *ton*, and Emily regaled her with stories of the neighborhood. They went for long walks, as they had been wont to do in their childhood, and spent many amusing evenings playing whist with the vicar and his wife.

When Simon was home, they both tried their best to stay out of his way.

"Why's the brat still here?" Clarissa overheard him asking Emily on the stairs one evening after he had returned relatively early from an outing with several of his friends.

"Shhh," Emily had said. "I forbid you to use such language to refer to my sister."

"True, she's not quite young enough to be a brat anymore," he slurred. "Bein' so long in the tooth an' all. Just wanted to know when she was leavin' to go up to the old hag's in Yorkshire."

"Simon!"

"Well, it's true, ain't it? Anyway, it's about time old Clare was on her way. We're in awfully dun territory to be takin' in guests. Your aunt can better handle her upkeep."

"Don't I have a right to visit with my own sister?"

"Why couldn't you wait 'til she was up in the north? Visit her there."

The couple had moved out of earshot then, leaving Clarissa seething as she lay in bed, wishing for sleep that would not come.

She hated being treated like a burdensome poor relation. But the situation would be no better at her Great-Aunt Agatha's, she knew. She had already had several letters from that redoubtable lady since arriving at Tuncliffe Manor, all of them redolent of the life awaiting her in Yorkshire. In her last letter, her great-aunt had rejoiced at the thought of Clarissa's imminent arrival. "Finally, someone I can rely on to massage my feet and prepare decent poultices," she had written. "And these witless maids have no idea how to run a house properly. I know you will be able to take the situation in hand. So considerate of your father to think of sending you to me, just in time for the harvest season."

Thank goodness Clarissa had found a way to avoid the life her father and great-aunt had mapped out for her. Not that there was any guarantee that her new life would be much of an improvement. She sighed again.

"Oh, Clare, do cheer up. I cannot abide seeing you so distressed." Emily's voice cut into her gloomy thoughts. "Shall we visit the vicarage today? Mrs. Humboldt's garden is looking so lovely this year."

"That would be marvelous," Clarissa replied with some degree of enthusiasm. "But we should return early, as I still have a few tasks to finish to prepare for tomorrow."

A shadow crossed Emily's face as she poured herself another cup of coffee. She motioned to the waiting footman, who withdrew from the room, leaving them alone.

"Must you truly go through with this mad plan?" she asked her sister in a low voice. "Life in the Canadas is quite unpleasant, I have heard. Surely it will be worse than living with Great-Aunt Agatha?"

"Perhaps, but at least I will have an opportunity to see new places and try to live an independent life. With Great-Aunt Agatha, I would be lucky to escape to London once every few years, and for the rest of the time I would be little more than an indentured servant."

"But won't you be just that once you take on the position as governess?" Emily was puzzled.

"In a manner of speaking, I suppose so. It is difficult to explain." Clarissa paused. "Perhaps the distinction lies simply in the degree of respect I would be accorded. I would rather work for an honest wage than be forever reminded of Great-Aunt Agatha's generosity in taking in a destitute relative." Her chin lifted slightly. "I have never wished to be a burden upon anyone."

"Oh, Clare," Emily interjected warmly. "I am certain she doesn't think of you that way. And if that is the issue, you are always welcome to stay here with us." Her voice faltered slightly, but her gaze was steady.

As they did so often these days, to her intense annoyance, Clarissa's eyes misted at this unexpected offer from her sister. "That is so kind of you, Emily, but we both know that is impossible. I could not live with myself knowing that I was the source of discord between you and Simon."

"There are many of sources of discord between myself and Simon. You need not worry about adding to them." Emily picked at a pulled thread in the tablecloth.

"I wish that I could make things better for you," Clarissa said impulsively. "You have always been so good to me."

"Oh, don't worry about me. I do tolerably well. Simon is absent most of the time, and I have my friends and some worthwhile, gratifying tasks. Really, it could be much worse. Marriage is not such an unmitigated horror. Are you certain you would not be willing to try it?"

"I am certain," said Clarissa with determination. "I seem unable to recognize a decent man when I am presented with one. No, I think I am much better suited to the spinster life."

Emily shook her head. "I doubt that, but there never was any arguing with you. But have you considered what Father will say when he hears you are gone?"

"By the time he hears, it will be too late to stop me in any case," Clarissa said sternly. "You did promise you would not tell anyone of my plan."

"I promised." Emily's voice was resigned.

"Father will say, in all likelihood, that he is well rid of an unwanted expense," Clarissa continued. "And do not worry that he will blame you for this escapade. I will write to him informing him that you did not know of my plans before I arrived here, and that you were most determined to change my mind." Clarissa smiled.

Emily's forehead was still furrowed with worry. "And you are certain that everything is arranged for your passage?"

"Miss Hilson's letter explained it all. I am to meet her at the docks in Southampton tomorrow afternoon. Everything is settled."

"I hope so," Emily said dubiously. "Would you like another cup of coffee?"

* * *

"My dear, you look just as fresh and lovely as I remember you at fourteen," exclaimed Miss Hilson delightedly.

"I hope I have matured somewhat since then," Clarissa replied with a laugh.

"Of course, of course! Although I certainly hope you have thought seriously about this decision. Once one emigrates to the Canadas, it is decidedly difficult to return."

"I have thought it through quite thoroughly. During the voyage, I am certain I will have ample opportunity to tell you the nature of my life over the last few months, and to explain why I feel this is the best course to pursue."

Her old schoolmistress had changed very little, Clarissa thought. She still wore her wavy dark hair pulled back neatly but not severely into a knot at the nape of her neck. Her clothes were still sober and plain, her laughter just as infectious, her personality still as outgoing. She would, Clarissa thought with satisfaction, make an excellent traveling companion.

Thoughts of traveling spurred her to again look at the ship on which they were to travel. The huge ship, the *Argosy,* lay at anchor, its half-furled sails flapping listlessly in the light breeze. Farther out into the harbor, Clarissa could see whitecaps. The voyage would take several weeks. The very thought made the bile rise in Clarissa's throat. She shuddered slightly.

To take her mind away from the coming voyage and its attendant horrors, she glanced about the area surrounding the docks. A half-dozen narrow cobblestone streets led from the busy wharf. The ruined medieval splendor of St. Michael's Church rose above the town. In the distance, she could see glimpses of the crumbling Norman walls that had once encircled the town. A tumble of homes, shops, and factories clustered around the busy shipping area. Somewhere in the distance, a church bell pealed faintly.

She would never see these shores again, she reflected sadly. She would never see her family again. Emily had refused to accompany her to Southampton.

"It's terrible enough that you are going," she had wept that morning. "I could not bear to stand on the wharf and watch you board the ship. Truly, I would feel compelled to hold you back."

And so they had said their heartfelt goodbyes in the drawing room of Tuncliffe Manor, as Simon looked on with undisguised relief. His expression only strengthened Clarissa's conviction that she was doing the right thing. Nothing in the Canadas could be as demeaning as spending one's life feeling beholden to uncaring relatives.

Simon's groom, having been sworn to secrecy, had conveyed her by carriage to the waterfront, seen her safely into the care of Miss Hilson and her party, and left.

"Will it soon be time to board the ship?" Clarissa asked.

Miss Hilson smiled at what she perceived to be her younger friend's impatience. "Any minute now."

* * *

"Good afternoon, my lord," said Emily Wallace with a self-possession she did not feel. Why on earth had this devastatingly handsome earl come to call now?

"Good afternoon, Lady Tuncliffe." Matthew Carstairs looked around the small room distractedly. "Would your sister, Lady Clarissa, be at home?"

"I am afraid you have just missed the chance of meeting her," replied Emily sadly. "She is gone."

"Gone? Gone where?"

Emily stared at her lap, playing with the folds of her sprigged muslin dress. What was she to say? She could not lie and say her sister had gone to Yorkshire. Nor, because of her promise to Clarissa, could she reveal her true destination. Quick thinking had never been her strong suit. She had not anticipated dealing with this dilemma so soon.

"Lady Tuncliffe?" Lord Langdon's voice was thick with barely concealed impatience.

Slowly, she raised her eyes. "She is simply gone, my lord. She made me promise that I would reveal no more than that."

"Has she gone to Yorkshire?"

She could not lie. Slowly, she shook her head.

"Then where? Where has she gone?"

"I don't wish to be impertinent, but why is my sister's destination of such vital import to you?" Emily struggled to deflect the conversation into less dangerous waters.

"I am simply concerned for her safety," Lord Langdon replied. "Did she go to Southampton?"

Emily could feel a dull flush crawling up her neck and cheeks. How she wished she could tell this man where Clarissa had gone! Perhaps he could force some sense upon her stubborn sister. But she had promised.

Langdon was observing her keenly from beneath dark brows. "You color so easily, just like your sister. It is all right, you do not need to tell me in words. It is obvious." He sagged against the chair dispiritedly. Emily noticed for the first time the mud on his boots and the dark smudges below his eyes. She suspected he had been riding all night.

"So I have missed her after all," he muttered, gazing abstractedly at his knees. "She has already sailed."

"I did not say that, my lord."

He looked up quickly. "That's true. You didn't."

"In fact, I did not promise to keep secret the fact that she left just a few hours ago."

A slow smile spread across Matthew's face. "You will forgive me, Lady Tuncliffe, if I depart rather hastily?"

Emily felt an answering smile at the corner of her own lips. "If you think it will do any good, my lord, please leave posthaste, with my blessing."

Matthew suddenly remembered Lightning. The animal had nearly dropped in exhaustion as they had drawn near to Tuncliffe Manor just minutes ago, after an all-night ride along dark highways from London. The beast was in no shape for a gallop into Southampton.

"My horse . . ." he began tentatively.

"My husband has several fine horses." Emily was brisk. "Please select a mount. Viking is the fastest."

So, only minutes after reining in in front of Tuncliffe Manor, Matthew found himself back in the saddle, this time on an elegant but rather skittish hunter.

Matthew had no time for the niceties of getting acquainted. With a light flick of the whip they were off, horse and rider thundering down the gravel drive in the direction of the port.

What on earth could she have been thinking, Matthew asked himself angrily as the horse's hooves pounded along the dusty road. For a gently bred young woman to undertake such a journey—it was completely cloth-headed! He wondered at her former schoolmistress for encouraging such madness. And Clarissa was prone to seasickness, on top of everything else. By the time she landed at Halifax she would be a sorry sight indeed.

But, he had to admit as he spurred the horse forward, he was not only concerned about Clarissa. The fact he had not wanted to face throughout the long trip from London finally seeped into his head as he thundered along the road to Southampton. He was equally concerned about the thought of never seeing her again.

Since leaving Denham House the day before, he had not given himself time or permission to ponder the reasons behind his precipitous trip to Hampshire. If asked, he would have said he simply wanted to save a young woman from making a tremendous mistake.

And yet, he suspected that Clarissa could survive quite well in the Canadas. Naive she was, and stubborn. But a fearful, missish mouse she was not. If she was determined to carve out a life for herself in the colonies, he had no doubt she could do just that.

No, he finally admitted as he saw the spires of Southampton arising in the hazy distance, his main motivation for running her to earth was not to stop her from going to the colonies. It was to stop her from leaving his life. The more time he had spent with Miss Isabella Larkin, the more he had realized he could not sentence himself to that sort of marriage. He and Clarissa had sparred, of course. They had argued more often than they had enjoyed peaceful company. She had discounted his advice, embarrassed him over her father's dinner table, disparaged his motivations. Why then, could he not get her out of his mind?

Perhaps, just perhaps, he loved her.

He groaned loudly. That was the last thing he needed. Had he not spent his entire adult life trying to avoid the trap that had ensnared his uncle and aunt?

Resolutely, he blocked the thought from his mind and urged the horse faster toward Southampton.

# SIXTEEN

"All ashore who's goin' ashore!" yelled a voice high above their heads on the deck of the *Argosy*.

"Well, Clarissa, are you ready for our adventure?" Miss Hilson's smile was so warm, Clarissa couldn't let the misery she felt creeping over her to show.

"I can hardly wait to see my first moose," she said with an enthusiasm she did not, at that moment, feel. She followed Miss Hilson tentatively up the gangplank, trying not to look below her at the lapping water nor to notice the swaying of the boards beneath her feet. She said a silent prayer that she would survive the inevitable seasickness intact.

And then she thought she heard someone calling her name.

"Impossible!" she admonished herself sternly. No one but Emily and Miss Hilson knew she was here, and both had been sworn to secrecy.

"Clarissa!" came the cry again, louder now. Clarissa knew for a fact that she was fantasizing, because the shout came in Lord Langdon's voice. And he was the last person on earth who would come to wish her bon voyage.

Miss Hilson touched her gently on the shoulder.

"Were you expecting anyone to come to see you off, my dear? There's a gentleman riding down that street to our left, and he seems most anxious to get your attention."

Clarissa turned and, to her astonishment, saw Matthew hurtling toward the docks on an elegant black stallion that looked suspiciously like Simon's prize hunter, Viking. What on earth . . . ?

"For God's sake, Clarissa!" he cried. Heads on the wharf swiveled in his direction.

What happened next would always seem blurred to Clarissa, like events observed through a dirty window during a thunderstorm. She noticed a stevedore rolling a large barrel along the wharf just in front of the street down which Matthew was riding. He obviously didn't hear the rapidly approaching rider. Oh no, she thought wildly. Oh no.

"Matthew!" she screamed, breaking through the people swarming along the gangplank. "Matthew, stop!"

But it was too late. Matthew and Viking galloped out of the alley as though propelled by a slingshot. The terrified stevedore leaped out of the way of Viking's pounding hooves, but lost his grip on the barrel. The barrel rolled in front of the huge stallion. Viking reared up dangerously, throwing Matthew to the cobblestones.

Heedless of the frankly curious stares, Clarissa fought her way through the people queuing up to board the ship, Miss Hilson close behind her.

"No, please go back, you'll miss the sailing," Clarissa gasped as she raced blindly toward the frantic horse and its motionless rider. "Please, Miss Hilson, I will be all right. But I can't go now." She turned to face the older woman. "I can't go now," she repeated foolishly. "But thank you so much for everything." She quickly hugged her startled companion and broke into a run across the wharf, her attention focused solely on Matthew's crumpled body.

Her friend watched her go, and then hailed one of the ship's officers and launched into a hasty conversation.

A crowd was gathering around the fallen man. With a brusqueness and strength she had not known she possessed, Clarissa forced her way through the throng. "Please, please stand back," she panted. "Does anyone know where I might find a physician?"

"Too late for that, ma'am," said a thin young man at the edge of the crowd. "Looks to me as though he's . . ."

"Shush!" admonished a huge woman with unruly gray hair. "Let her see fer herse'f."

Her heart thundering in her chest, Clarissa knelt by Matthew's side. His face was an unhealthy shade of gray, and his left leg was cruelly twisted beneath him, but after a few seconds of close observation she saw that he was still breathing. Shallowly.

"It is not too late," she said crisply, rising and surveying the crowd. She reached into her reticule and withdrew a few shillings. "Will someone please fetch the nearest physician?"

"I will, ma'am." It was the same young man who had tried to tell her that Matthew was dead. "I'm sorry 'bout what I said, ma'am."

"Just be as quick as you can," Clarissa said distractedly, handing him the coins for his trouble. He was off like a shot.

"And please, everyone, stand back. Give him room to breathe," she pleaded. The crowd moved back a few paces.

"Lord Langdon," she murmured as she knelt again. Forgetting all claims of etiquette, she continued more urgently. "Matthew. Matthew! You're going to be all right. The physician is coming. You will be fine." She doubted he could hear her, and doubted the truth of her own words. But she felt compelled to keep talking, a torrent of phrases to block out other thoughts.

And yet, they still crept in. Why was Matthew here? Had her father sent him? What would happen to her now? And, most importantly, would he really be all right?

Clarissa had no idea how long she had been murmuring to the unconscious earl, but eventually her messenger returned with a panting, elderly man whose leathery cheeks were flushed with exertion.

"Oh my," he muttered, slowly lowering himself down beside Matthew.

Quietly and efficiently he examined the prone man. Clarissa looked away when the doctor lifted Matthew's head from the cobbles and revealed a sticky pool of blood beneath.

"Don't worry, ma'am, it's just a flesh wound. There's no bump. He's just scraped his head against something. It's his arm and leg that have taken most of the impact of the fall." He looked at her curiously. "Who is the gentleman? And are you his wife?"

"He is the Earl of Langdon," she said dully. A murmur ran through the crowd. "And no, I am not his wife. Just a friend."

"A very concerned friend, I can see," said the older man kindly.

"Will he be all right?" she said in the same lifeless voice.

The physician pursed his lips. "I don't want to lie to you, ma'am. He has taken a terrible fall. But I do not think his unconscious state is deep, and his leg, thankfully, is not broken." He paused. "Do you live in Southampton?"

"No, neither myself nor the earl are from this area. However, my sister lives not far away. Perhaps you know her—Lady Tuncliffe?"

"Ah yes, I have met her. A lovely person."

"Would it be possible to remove Lord Langdon to Tuncliffe Manor?" Clarissa was certain that her return, with an invalid, would not be greeted with enthusiasm on her brother-in-law's part, but it appeared to be her only alternative.

The physician, however, was shaking his head. "I do not believe that would be wise, Lady . . . ?" His eyebrows rose slightly.

"Lady Clarissa Denham," she said quickly, ignoring the social niceties of introductions.

"Pleased to make your acquaintance. I am Dr. Sam Watkins. We must get this man's wounds cleaned and dressed, and put him to bed somewhere warm and dry." He looked at her questioningly.

"Is there a respectable inn nearby?" she asked.

"Why yes, the Lion's Head is run by a friend of

mine. It is not far." He paused uncertainly. "Are you alone, my lady?"

Clarissa suddenly realized the awkwardness of the situation. But there was nothing for it. Matthew had to be attended to, and quickly. "Yes, I . . ."

"Lady Clarissa!" called an unknown voice.

She turned to watch a middle-aged, red-haired man in a respectable if somewhat threadbare suit of clothes approaching. "Lady Clarissa!" he said again as he reached her side. She noted his marked Irish accent. "My name is Tim Hanlon, and I'm a friend of Cap'n Jamieson's. He's after sendin' me along to keep an eye on you."

"Captain Jamieson? To keep an eye on me?" Clarissa repeated stupidly.

"Your friend there, the lady with the dark hair? She told the bos'un that she had to leave, but she was desperately worried about you. He called the cap'n, and she gave Jamieson some money and asked him for help. I was down helpin' out on the *Argosy* before it sailed, so he asked me." He paused, clearly uncertain what to do next. "So, is there anything I can do?"

Clarissa was touched by Miss Hilson's concern for her welfare. As it turned out, Tim Hanlon's presence would give her just the veneer of respectability she needed. She smiled warmly.

"Yes, Tim, there is. If you could help Dr. Watkins move this gentleman to the Lion's Head Inn, I would very much appreciate it. And later, there may be other tasks you can assist me with, if it wouldn't be too much trouble."

"No trouble at all, my lady," replied Tim Hanlon firmly. "Your friend was quite generous."

Miss Hilson was truly one of a kind, Clarissa reflected. She hoped her friend would not encounter too many difficulties in the Canadas when she landed without the additional governess she had promised to bring.

But there was no time to think about that now. Dr. Watkins and Tim Hanlon were already preparing to move Matthew to the inn.

The dim light of dawn was filtering into the room when Matthew finally opened his eyes. He groaned.

A red-haired man, who was dozing in a chair by the fire, stirred to life as well. "Good morning, m'lord," he said in a pronounced brogue.

Matthew stared at him in bleary confusion.

"Don't worry yerse'f about me. I'm no one important. Rest there for a minute, and I'll be back." The stranger quickly left the room.

As the door closed behind the Irishman, Matthew sat forward and shook his head in an attempt to clear it. A knife blade of pain shot down his neck and he fell back against the pillows. What the devil had happened?

He remembered riding hellbent for leather down the steep street toward the wharf in Southampton. In his mind's eye, he saw Clarissa boarding the *Argosy*, oblivious to his shouts. Then something startled that skittish hunter of Tuncliffe's. The details became somewhat hazy after that.

So Clarissa really had gone. Well, it served him right. He was lying in bed in what appeared to be an inn, broken and bruised. That's what happens when one lets one's passions get away with oneself, he told himself wearily. His idiotic gallop from London to Hampshire had netted him nothing but pain. After spending his entire life avoiding impetuous acts, he had given in to an impulse and received a dented head and not much else for his trouble.

Perhaps, after all, he really was better off with a simpering miss like Isabella Larkin. She would certainly never inspire him to such acts of heedless recklessness.

He wondered how Clarissa was handling the sea voyage. Would she be seasick? And would she truly be happy working as a governess in some wild colony? Well, it was the life she had chosen. She would have to live with it, just as he was having to live with the results of his foolishness.

The door opened and the red-haired Irishman came in. "I've brought ye a visitor, my lord. She wanted me to wake her as soon as ye stirred. She'd've stayed here herse'f, but the wee woman who owns the place wouldn't hear of it." He opened the door wider and Clarissa crept through it, leaving it open behind her. "I'll be outside the door, if ye need me." Silently, the Irishman left.

Clarissa, her hair tousled and her eyes heavy with sleep, moved immediately to the bedside. "Matthew! I am so happy to see you awake."

Matthew was again tempted to shake the cobwebs from his head, but knew better this time. He stared at her in some confusion. "But you are gone. You were boarding the *Argosy.*"

"I was hardly going to leave you bleeding on the cobblestones, now was I?" She was indignant.

"What has happened to me, exactly? Where are we? And who is our Irish friend?"

Slowly and clearly, she told him about the events at the wharf and his subsequent transfer to the Lion's Head Inn.

"And how long ago was all that?"

"Yesterday."

Yesterday. He shook his head again, and winced.

"You must have a terrible headache," she said, leaning forward with concern.

"That is putting it very mildly." His head felt as though it had been the ball at a particularly energetic cricket match.

"Well, the doctor will be most pleased to see you are conscious." She paused. "You have sprained your ankle, but he says that you should be top of the trees after a week of bed rest."

"A week?" Matthew mumbled. "I cannot stay here that long. I have responsibilities. My uncle, my estates . . . a speech next week in the Lords . . ."

"Those will all have to wait," she interrupted. "You will be going nowhere."

"I suppose it is exactly what I deserve," Matthew muttered.

"Pardon me?" Clarissa's eyebrows rose in surprise.

"Riding like a demon through a strange town on a strange horse. Not looking where I was going. Riding all night from London with no sleep and no food."

"You rode all night? Whatever for?"

"To keep you from throwing your life away on some buffleheaded expedition to the colonies," Matthew ground out.

"Ah, the brave knight coming to my rescue again," Clarissa said. Then she added hastily, "I do thank you for your concern, my lord. And I am so sorry that it led you into such an unfortunate accident."

"I behaved like a fool."

Clarissa said nothing, merely rose to her feet to stand by the window, which was pink with the growing light of day.

Seeing her standing there, when he had momentarily thought her gone forever to the Canadas, made his heart ache. Now, more than ever, he realized that he loved her. And now, more than ever, he knew that she was the worst possible woman in the world for him. His idiotic trip to Southampton had done no one any good. He had injured himself and some stranger's horse. He would be forced to put off his duties to his uncle, his tenants, and his colleagues in the House. Such mishaps and disturbances would only become more common if he was such a fool as to marry for love.

"Now that you are conscious again, and I can see for myself that you are out of danger, I will be on my way. Probably tomorrow." Clarissa spoke suddenly from her post by the window.

"Tomorrow?" he said, struggling to a sitting position. "Where on earth do you plan to go?"

She continued to gaze abstractedly out the window, but he heard her sigh. "Where else am I to go? My chance to go to the Canadas is lost. Neither my sister nor my mother can keep me. My father has made it plain that he won't keep me. Only my great-aunt seems to have any use for my presence. I will leave for Yorkshire on tomorrow's stage."

"On the stage . . .!" he bellowed.

"Yes, on the stage," she replied, her voice crisp. "Unlike some of us, I am not lord of one of England's richest estates. As the poor relation forced to depend on the kindness of other family members, I hardly think it would be appropriate for me to arrive in a coach-and-four. Do you?"

For the first time, he realized how demeaning this entire arrangement was to her. He tried to put himself in her place. What if he had been sent by his family to act as little better than an indentured servant for a crotchety relative? What if he had grasped at freedom, only to see it fall away through his fingers?

He could not allow himself to become sentimental about her. It would only lead to ruin.

But he could not let her leave a second time, either.

"There is another alternative," he said softly.

She did not turn from the window. "Believe me, my lord, I would be most glad to hear it."

"I am afraid the circumstances are no better than they were the first time I asked you this," he began slowly. "But I will ask it again. Will you do me the honor, Clarissa, of becoming my wife?"

That made her turn around, he noted with satisfaction. But the expression on her face was anything but pleasing.

"Please don't do this," she murmured. "Above all else, I could not bear it if I thought you felt sorry for me."

"Felt sorry for you? Do you think I go about making offers for young women because I feel sorry for them?" His head throbbed, but he didn't care.

"Now that you mention offers, have you not already offered for Miss Larkin?"

"No, now that you mention it, I have not."

"Why not? You told me some weeks ago that a betrothal was imminent."

"There was an impediment."

She looked at him with unmasked surprise. "What was that?"

"You."

She began to pace the room in agitation. "What is it that you want of me, my lord? Why can you not just leave me alone? I have made it clear to you time and again that I have no wish to live in a loveless marriage, and you have made it clear to me as many times that a love match is the furthest possible thing from your desires. I believe that puts us at something of an impasse." She glared at him.

"My thoughts on the matter have changed." Tired, he leaned back against the pillows. Now that he had voiced his offer, he knew he wanted her to say yes more than he had ever wanted anything in his life. But he wanted her to say yes with a loving heart.

"How have your thoughts changed, my lord?" She continued to pace.

"Why do you think I rode out here like one of the Four Horsemen of the Apocalypse to keep you from getting on that ship? And stop saying 'my lord'," he added irrelevantly.

"You have already explained why you came here. You felt some sort of unfathomable desire to rescue me." Her eyes were unreadable.

He gave up the effort to be urbane and detached. He was too tired. "It was not an unfathomable desire. I did it because I love you. It frightens me beyond words, but I love you."

She sat down on a chair, speechless.

"I know you do not love me," he continued. "But I could make you comfortable. You would not have to live with your aunt . . ."

"When did I ever say that I did not love you?" Her voice, rich with challenge, startled him.

"When did you say you did?"

"I am saying it now."

His heart swelled with an exultation like none he had ever experienced before. "I didn't hear you," he said playfully.

"I love you, Matthew."

"There, that's better." He smiled with satisfaction, and beckoned her to sit next to him on the bed.

She sat beside him. He picked up her hand and raised it softly to his lips. "Now, about my question . . ."

"Yes, Matthew. Yes. I will marry you."

He drew her into his arms for a long and lingering kiss. "You've become remarkably agreeable of late," he said with a laugh as they finally drew apart.

"It will not last, my lord," she said with a smile.

"I know that," he said. "I should become bored if it did."

# About the Author

Laura Paquet lives with her husband and two in-sane cats in Ottawa, Canada. *Lord Langdon's Tutor* is her first Regency romance. She would love to hear from her readers. Please write to her at 390 Rideau Street, P.O. Box 20019, Ottawa, Ontario, Canada K1N 9N5, or send her an e-mail at laura@corner-stoneword.com. And please visit her web site at www.LauraByrnePaquet.com for news of signings and upcoming books.

# More Zebra Regency Romances